GIVEN NAMES

STUART FABE

Author's Note

HAVE YOU EVER THOUGHT ABOUT what you'd do if you won the lottery? I mean, like an astronomical figure north of two hundred million dollars. Who would you tell? Who would you trust to manage your money? What would you buy? And, how much would you give away and to whom?

Most of us might simply say, "Just give me the dough, and I'm sure I can figure it out." Truth is, I doubt many of us would really know the answers to those questions until we were faced with such a stunning windfall, and then it begs the existential question: How would it change your life?

These are the issues that Nathan Andrews confronts as he barrels headlong into great wealth and faces sudden questions about his personal relationships, who he is, and what his life is all about.

Given Names isn't meant to be a didactic, self-help book intended to show people "the way." I've written it purely for entertainment. The beauty about all of the questions that Nathan contends with, and the people whose lives he conjoins, is that my readers have an opportunity to face their own wonderings; to look at themselves in the mirror with a clear eye and determine where their priorities lie.

Given Names is my tenth novel, and I've written it as a stand-alone literary work. I've planned no sequels other than my life, itself, which brings enough questions and hopefully ample answers so that someday when I exit this world, the person I've seen in the mirror will nod his approval at how I lived my life.

I hope you enjoy this story and find some clarity of thought along the way. Indeed, we need not win the lottery to craft our enduring legacies, but then again, wouldn't it be nice?!

— Stuart Fabe
Greencastle, Indiana

Dedication

In Loving Memory Of
Brian David Helton
Father, Son, Brother, and Friend

And For

Reverend Bryan Langdoc and Beth Benedix
Inspirational Friends Who See Farther
by Standing on the Shoulders of Giants

Prologue

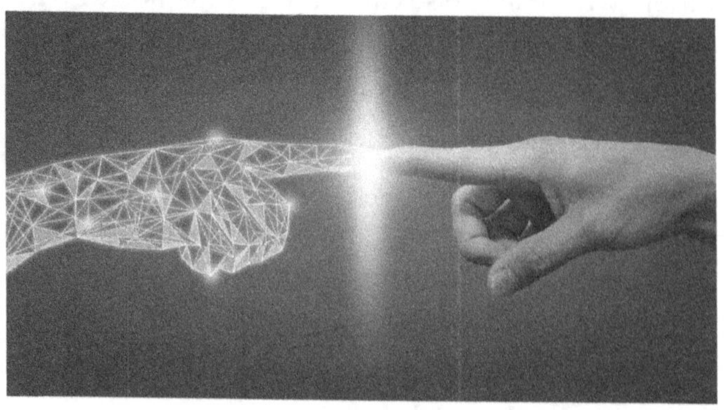

'VE NEVER CONSIDERED MYSELF to be a very lucky guy. Sure, I came from a loving family that valued education, and I'm very fortunate to enjoy reasonably good health, but as far as winning really big stuff, well, that's something that happens to other people.

In retrospect, growing up in the Camelot-like neighborhood called Rose Hill in Cincinnati, Ohio, I ran with many kids who came from very well-heeled families whose parents were physicians, lawyers, business owners, corporate executives, and several others whose largesse came the old-fashioned way: They inherited it. Talk about winning the lottery without even buying a ticket!

But early on I came to also realize that having a lot of dough was a double-edged sword. Granted, my closest friend's parents owned a Picasso painting, a Henry Moore sculpture, a Jaguar XKE, and a lake house in Northern Michigan…all pretty cool stuff, but fortunately even as a young man I recognized that a few of the "rich kids" I grew up with were also amiable doofuses. I learned quickly that family wealth didn't inoculate them from frivolity, lethargy, and mediocrity. Sure, I appreciated the trappings of their family wealth, but I was more impressed by what many of these people knew that allowed them to acquire such affluence.

Conversely, my mother and father were born to immigrant parents who arrived in America in the 1910s from Zhytomyr, Ukraine, and other shtetls across Eastern Europe. My grandparents' English was heavily accented, and they didn't have two nickels to rub together when they got off the boat. To their credit, they kicked the doors of their former lives shut and never looked back. "We're Americans now!"

My parents were wonderful people. Dad was a very talented artist who attended the Art Students League in New York and somehow survived five years in the army during World War II, including landing in Normandy on D-Day and surviving the terrifying Battle of the Bulge. When he returned to the States in 1945, he regained his humanity by painting landscapes and city scenes populated with brightly clad children, and eventually he became a beloved art professor at the University of Cincinnati.

My mother, Miriam, was a devoted stay-at-home mom looking after my brother and me. Despite her quietly taking a back seat to my father's rather healthy ego, Mom was the best part of our family; the glue that kept us healthy, educated, and focused on being positive, constructive human beings. She had come from a very small town in Kentucky along the Ohio River, the only Jewish kid around for miles, and despite her shyness and modest education, she truly was a woman of valor. She put everyone in the family before herself, and to this day, I view her as the best of the bunch. As for me, my name's Nathan Andrews, and I'm a writer and photographer. I didn't start out that way, though. Matter of fact, I didn't know what I wanted to do with my life during and immediately after college. There was a lot of social turmoil during the sixties, and one thing I knew for sure was that I didn't want to get drafted and shipped off to Vietnam. So, I majored in English literature for reasons I still don't quite understand and juggled my academic hours to remain a full-time student instead of a statistic in the killing fields of Southeast Asia. Back in those days "the lottery" had a totally different meaning for those of us who were draft age, and I guess I actually was a very lucky guy because my number never got called. Alas, fifty-five thousand American lives later the war in Vietnam came to an inglorious end. Such a long time ago, now …

In the early years of my career, I worked with young people who came from ghettos and less-fortunate neighborhoods, first as a wide-eyed employee in one of President Johnson's Great Society programs, and then as a probation officer and program director with Hamilton County Juvenile Court in Cincinnati. I learned a lot of lessons in those early years. Working with many of those young people and their families, I witnessed the differences in their tough daily struggles versus the mere relative nuisances that my friends and I experienced growing up. It's curious, but as I think about it, I always remember my mother saying, "Be on the side of the underdog. Look out for the less fortunate. Be kind to women." Just positive-sounding words then. Golden wisdom in retrospect.

But, being the eager individual I was, I was lured away from my direct, hands-on career working with less fortunate folks to raising charitable funds for organizations that benefited them. In my heart I knew that my psyche wasn't in tune with the life of a social worker, but I knew that I had a knack for raising money and felt comfortable around people who had it. And, because raising dough paid better than the employees who directly worked with needy folks, I was able to do well and do good at the same time. Thus began my career as a full-time development executive for Children's Hospital Medical Center, The Jewish Hospital, and the Cincinnati Zoo and Botanical Garden…and man, was I ever fortunate to represent such fine institutions.

But, after raising charitable funds, day in and day out, for some thirty years, I was frankly burned-out and wondered what was next in store for me. That's when I went to an outdoor art fair at Coney Island along the Ohio River and ran headlong into my future, although I didn't know it at the time. I rounded a corner and stepped inside of a canopy, and there she was, looking like a contemporary pagan princess in a long flowing dress with hair the color of afternoon sunlight.

Her name was Marlita, and I overheard her telling a customer in her art booth that she'd recently lost her husband to cancer and lived alone on a quiet farm in west central Indiana. She was alone, that is, if you didn't count the two dogs, two cats, assorted field mice, a scattering of ladybugs, and a myriad of songbirds that warmly greeted her presence and counted on her to nurture them through harsh seasons. And, she was alone only if you forgot the wind that shimmered through the grasses and rippled the surface of her pond, or if you dismissed the fields laden with Buddha-shaped gourds that she grew and decorated and made her living selling. And, she was never alone when her two grown sons visited the farmhouse and doted on their mother, sometimes as strong young men, other times as needy boys. They had lost their father, and she her husband, and their hearts bore open wounds. And yet, with everything and everyone around her, Marlita was seemingly very alone now in a blue frame farmhouse, on thirty-six acres of rolling pasture, down six miles of quiet country roads near the town of Greencastle, Indiana.

And, when I saw her at the art fair, I was so mesmerized by this golden-haired country lass that thoughts of my former life vanished like smoke in the wind. I knew that come what may, it was time for a major change …

And, change it did. Marlita and I stayed in touch, and two years later I sold my house in the tony neighborhood of Hyde Park. I quit my six-figure job, ditched my suits, my monogrammed shirts and cuff links, and became a country fella living in a blue frame farmhouse with the prettiest girl on the planet.

When I arrived in the Putnam County country-side, I brought several of my belongings with me; the most treasured of which were my antique brass bed, my collection of vintage cameras, a large portfolio of my photographs, and my photographic equipment. It was a very curious process deciding which items to bring with me to my new life and which to ditch. In some ways I felt like an immigrant arriving in a new world, not unlike my grandparents, each of us "strangers in a strange land." We kicked the doors of our past lives shut and didn't look back.

Marlita soon transitioned from traveling to art fairs selling her attractive gourd art to teaching yoga in a lovely, spacious studio that I had built onto our old dairy barn after I sold much of my camera collection. She became enthralled with her new life, and I had to conjure up the next iteration of mine. Fortunately, being a rather resourceful country gent, I came up with ways to keep myself engaged in life while living in the middle of absolutely nowhere. So, I learned about photographing the night sky and began writing suspense stories… and basically repurposed my life in ways I never expected.

I could go on and on about my rapture with the night sky. I mean, who couldn't, right? When I go outside and look up and see the galactic core of the Milky Way, or the moon, or distant planets and shooting stars, I feel closer to any deity than I ever have. And, then I take the photographs and enhance them on my computer to maximize their radiant details…and voila! A perfect way to remember a great night under the stars. I'll leave astrophysics to the scientists. I'm delighted to be swept away by the night sky's majesty, and all I have to do is go outside at night with my gear and look up.

As for writing suspense novels, I never really know what story lines or characters will flow from my fluid imagination onto my computer screen. The process just unfolds, often slowly at first, and then it soon takes on a life of its own. At this point I've enjoyed writing and publishing ten novels and a similar number of photography and art books. Each book has a story to tell, and over time I've honed my work with increasingly satisfying results. In some ways the mystery of writing fictional stories isn't much different than peering into the wonders of the night sky. My plots and characters begin like random stars in an abstract universe that eventually coalesce into constellations, and finally a story is born from a slurry of cerebral dust and gases. The beauty is that I never know where my mind will travel next …

Chapter One

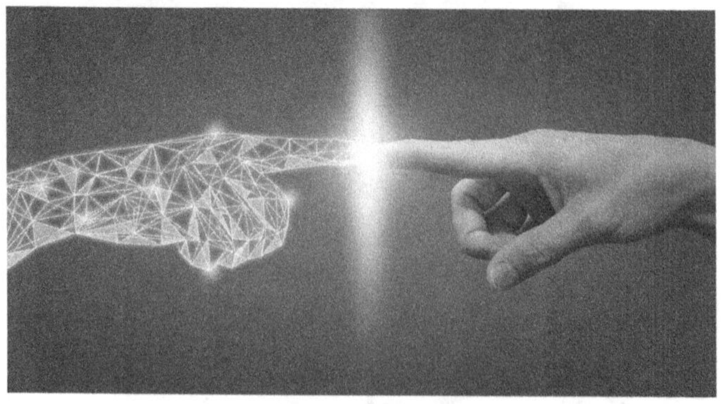

Present Day
Greencastle, Indiana

"NATHAN! Nathan, where are you?!"

"I'm up here in my office, honey. C'mon up!" I hear Marlita climb the steps to the second floor of our home and see her lovely face peer through my half-open office door just off of our bedroom. I swear, we've been together for nearly twenty years now, but seeing her sparkling brown eyes still makes me smile. I'm a darn lucky guy!

"There you are!" she says a little out of breath. "What're you working on?"

"Oh, just noodling around on a story idea that I've been thinking about for a while."

"Cool! Think you've got something exciting for a new novel?"

"I think so, but I need to flesh out the details a bit more before diving in fully. What've you been up to this morning?"

"Well, I spent some time behind the barn preparing our raised garden beds for spring planting, and I just got off the phone with Linda and BJ."

"And, how're your sisters doing down in Florida? Enjoying warmer April weather than we are, no doubt."

"Yeah, they're fine. We're talking about taking another 'sissies vacation' together if that's okay with you."

"Oh boy! Look out world, the Stanley sisters are about to descend on you again! So, where are you thinking about going this time and when do you think you'll go?"

Marlita leans against me affectionately and asks, "Are you sure you don't mind my leaving you for a little while? We're trying to decide between going to the Maldives or perhaps Greece and Croatia."

"Wow, they all sound like great destinations. Which are you leaning toward?"

"I've always wanted to go to Greece and Croatia, and I think Linda and BJ are excited about going there too. As to when we'd go, I showed them some last-minute travel packages online, and we can get some great deals flying to Athens and then on to Dubrovnik, like as soon as next week." She winces a little thinking I might be upset by the sudden soon departure time and is relieved when I say, "There's a lot to be said for spontaneity. I'm fine with whatever travel plans you girls choose to make. I've got enough yard work and writing to keep me occupied while you're away. How long do you think you'd be gone?"

"Really!? Seriously, Nathan, you don't mind if we go that soon?" She winces a little again and says, "We'd probably be gone for about three weeks."

"Three weeks!" I declare in mock protest. "That's an eternity!" I give her a big hug and add, "That's fine, darlin', you know I'm all in favor of you and your sisters traveling together. I mean, life's not a dress rehearsal, right, and time's moving on for all of us. I think that became even clearer when the two of them lost their husbands. So, yeah, go and enjoy yourselves, and don't fret about me. I can always rummage around in the freezer for one of the healthy meals you've got tucked away, plus I'm perfectly capable of finding something not-so-healthy to eat at the grocery store or at the Monon Diner. Stella's always willing to have her kitchen prepare whatever I want."

"Seriously, Nathan, you're okay with my leaving you for a while?"

"You know I am. I want you to enjoy life to the fullest, but I must say that you three Stanley girls unleashed on an unsuspecting world is a mighty frightening thought."

She pokes me in the ribs, and shouts as she scoots away, "I've got to get my sissies on the phone again. We've got plans to make. Thank you, my love!" And, she's gone!

I shake my head in amusement and look at my plump cat, Bella, who's taken up a prone position on my desk between me and my keyboard.

"Well, Bella, looks like it's going to be just you and me again for a while. Think you can handle my amazing jokes and witty repartee for three weeks?" She responds by totally ignoring me in favor of a ladybug that's just landed near her outstretched paw. So much for her undivided attention! I gently slide her off my desk and stare at my computer screen again trying to regain my creative mojo, but for now my, uh, literary brilliance has gone bye bye.

"Wow, three weeks," I whisper to myself. "I wonder what mischief I can get into while my sweet Marlita is an ocean and a continent away."

Through my floor register I can hear Marlita's muffled laughter one floor below me in her office. She didn't waste any time reconnecting with her sisters on a Zoom call, and they're makin' plans! I can't make out exactly what she's saying, but it's obvious that "the sissies" are chattering away. Frankly, I have no idea how they decide who speaks and who listens, but it works for them. They're always very sweet to invite me to tag along whenever they take a trip, and while we've done it very successfully before, I think it's just better for them to be an unescorted trio on their adventures.

I look around my office for Bella, but she's gone off in favor of either more entertaining company or a sunny window seat where she can survey her queendom. I sit at my desk and look at the very early pages of my new novel, but I know in my heart of hearts that I haven't totally invested in the story I've been working on. It's got potential, but I keep thinking that there's got to be a deeper story that's time for me to tell right now. During my previous nine novels I've scratched a lot of personal itches with suspense and supernatural elements; now I keep thinking that I want something different, no more murder and supernatural stuff, well, maybe a little, but something more personal.

I turn my computer off and look around my office. There is a lifetime of memories here, each one a story unto itself: Fossils that I collected from creek beds growing up, books spanning a broad range of subjects and images, furniture and antiques that I've owned for decades, wonderful paintings by my father that almost feel like siblings to me, endearing photos of our family, and night sky photographs that I'm especially fond of. This room, this study is my inner sanctum.

Fortunately, I traveled North America, Europe, Africa, and the Mediterranean extensively in years gone by, because at this point in my life I'm perfectly happy to hang out here on our property in the country and let my creative juices and the internet transport me to wherever I want to go. I'm not embarrassed to say that I've adopted a bit of a Hobbit-like lifestyle in my later years. I'm a Taurus, after all, and that's another excuse I use for being a homebody. I'll never forget my father counseling me: "Learn to create your own excitement and be content spending time by yourself. Creativity is a monastic-like experience." And happily, I've grown comfortable with the wisdom of those phrases over the years.

"Are you still in your study?" I hear Marlita shout up to me.

"Yeah, just wrapping a few things up."

"We're set!" she continues. "We've made our airline reservations and reserved our lodgings in Greece, and we're waiting for confirmation from places in Croatia. We leave Tuesday."

"Wow, that was quick!" I reply.

"Well, you know us. We are can-do girls! We got a terrific deal on last-minute airline reservations, and

I managed to sweet-talk the booking agent down on the price of our hotels while we're in Greece. Now, I have to reach out to my yoga students to let them know I'm canceling classes while I'm gone, and I've got a bunch of other things to do too. Are you all right being on your own for lunch?"

"Sure, I was thinking of running to the grocery store anyway, and I can stop by Stella's diner for lunch while I'm out."

Fifteen minutes later I've cleaned up a bit and put on some fresh clothes. I climb into my aging Tacoma pickup truck that I've nicknamed Pappy and pull out of our gravel driveway onto our county road. I immediately see our new neighbors, Phil and Erin Lindell, playing with their children in their large field across the road from our home. For years Marlita and I cringed at the thought of a new home being built across the way from us, but it's a beautiful home, and the Lindells and their three young kids are delightful. We're very fortunate to have them as neighbors!

The ride into the center of town is only six miles, along which there aren't any traffic lights and only one stop sign. Talk about the good life! I slowly drive past Drew Greenfield's pasture and see his flock of sheep grazing on lush, verdant grass. Drew's also my accountant, but he and his wife, Alicia, have also tended a sizable flock of sheep for many years. Alicia retired as an elementary school principal and is a highly regarded flutist. One of the early lessons I learned when I moved away from Cincinnati twenty years ago is that you never know what talents some people have living in the middle of nowhere. People can surprise us if we only let them!

I reach the one-lane bridge spanning the creek running alongside the Greenfields' property and stop to take a gander at the view. It's a charming little creek, strewn with rocks and bordered on both sides by walnut, locust, and sycamore trees. There's an old country lane that runs along the creek, and Marlita and I have spent many wonderful hours walking into its shade and solitude. Like I said, "It's a good life."

Next up is Don and Lisa Brand's spread, and I see Don in his barnyard working with a couple of his horses. I notice his chainsaw resting on a pile of freshly cut wood and make a mental note to text him about delivering another load of firewood if he's amenable. I lightly tap my horn and give him a wave as I slowly cruise past his property. After that, I really don't know many of the other folks living on the way to Greencastle. Most of the homes are modest-looking, and it's not unusual to see a woman walking a donkey or kids playing with their pet chickens and goats. Pretty dang wholesome!

Even though it's a short drive to town, the scarcity of traffic gives me an opportunity to look around and let my mind absorb things. The first half of the drive is through the country, and there's always something fascinating to see. Deer are plentiful and glimpsing wild turkeys and hawks always captures my attention. Once I get on State Route 231, I see a lot less wildlife and a lot more cropland and structures. The drive down Waterworks Hill and over Big Walnut Creek is a brief but visually appealing drive. The color of the creek water is always in a state of flux; sparkling slate gray, muddy brown, and sometimes a bluish teal. It all depends on the amount of rain that's fallen. Every rural community should have a creek like our Big Walnut, self-sustaining and yet protected by local conservationists.

I cruise past our Putnam County Fairgrounds and think about the large number of 4-H kids that are enthusiastically caring for their livestock and fine-tuning their projects. July will be here before you know it, and much of our community will take a break from normal routines to support the farmers and kids, and of course, enjoy the traditional fair food. Marlita and I always go, and this ol' city feller grins like a happy puppy when we visit the livestock barns and see the amazing vintage tractors on display. It's a totally different world than what I was exposed to in Cincinnati. I love the fair, even the odor!

I drive over the railroad tracks at the north edge of town and smile as I always do when I see the grand J.J. Hunter caboose sidelined near the Monon Diner. I mean, if you can't get excited seeing an old wooden caboose, well, you're just not-right-in-the-head! Okay, that's rude of me and not very politically correct, but you catch my drift, right?

I guide my pickup into a parking space at the side of the diner and turn off Pappy's engine. I'm not surprised that the parking lot is fairly full at lunchtime, and I'm not surprised that a bunch of the vehicles are pickup trucks. I mean, Greencastle is a lovely, vibrant little city, but when you get beyond the city limits in any direction, we're a farming community at heart, with deep roots … and pickups are the vehicles of choice.

Chapter Two

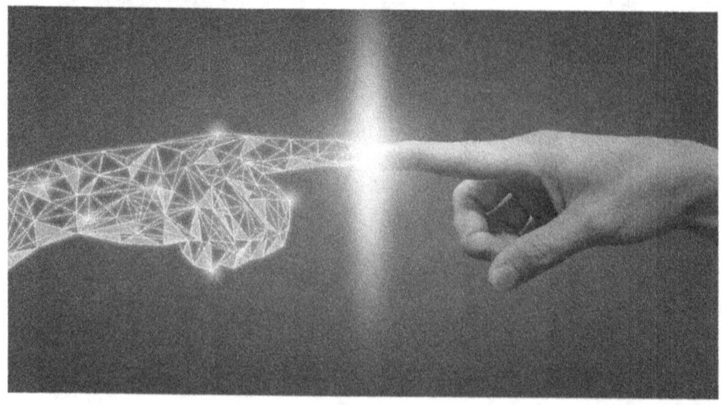

THE MONON DINER is a legendary Greencastle landmark. For many years it provided meals for local folks and passing railroad men. Then, when Sven Rudd up and passed away a while back, it lay fallow for perhaps five years until my friend Stella Chastain decided to resurrect it into a fine, down-home eatery. And, thank goodness for that because there's no restaurant food I like more than wholesome diner food! What can I say? I'm a complex dude with rather simple tastes.

As I reach the front door, I hold it open for an elderly couple who are exiting. I overhear the woman whisper to her husband: "That's Nathan Andrews."

I can't help but smile when I hear him reply, "So, who the hell's Nathan Andrews?!"

"He's that smart writer feller that lives north of town with that pretty girl who's a yoga instructor."

"He didn't look that smart to me," Rufus declares. "And, I just ate so why would I want some yogurt?!"

"I swear Rufus we need to get your hearing aids checked!"

"Maude, I didn't pay with a check. I gave 'em cash. I swear sometimes I wonder about your hearing."

Maude shakes her head in disbelief and helps guide her husband to their car. I watch as they struggle to get settled in their Buick, and thankfully, I see Maude take the wheel. Aging ain't for sissies, that's for sure!

I turn to enter the diner but end up holding the door open again for a couple of good ol' boys, one of whom burps odoriferously just as he passes me. Finally, I make it through the front door, and

I'm greeted by two wonderful sensory experiences: First, are the aromas coming from the kitchen, and secondly, is the sight of the owner of the Monon Diner and my good friend Stella.

"Well, if it's not my favorite author!" she coos as she gives me a warm hug. "So, where's Marlita or are you dining alone today?"

"Marlita's home getting ready to take another grand adventure with her two sisters. So, I'm flying solo today."

"Wow, those Stanley girls aren't letting any moss grow on them, are they? Where are they off to this time?"

"Greece and Croatia. They're leaving Tuesday and will be gone for about three weeks, so you may be seeing quite a bit of me."

Stella walks me over to a booth by the window, pours some coffee, and asks, "You having the usual, Nathan?"

"I already had breakfast, Stella, so I think I'll have your deluxe BLT on whole wheat toast and fries."

"Coming right up!" she replies and then scurries off to the cash register to collect dough from several of her satisfied customers who're lined up waiting to pay. I settle in, take a couple sips of coffee, and glance around at the diner's denizens who are actually a fairly diverse potpourri of Greencastle's populace today. Our fine mayor, Susan David, is in what appears to be a serious conversation with our *Banner* newspaper editor, Red Jergens. There are also several students from our Asbury College, a few ladies whom I've noticed here before, and a bunch of townspeople and farmers whose faces I've seen, but whose names escape me now.

I fill the time waiting for my lunch by reading assorted articles on my iPhone. The international news about Ukraine's war with Russia is truly heartbreaking, and our national news isn't much more mollifying. The local news is pretty much the same wholesome stuff about high school sports and upcoming events. For the first several years that I lived in the Putnam County countryside, I smugly looked down my nose at the *Banner's* news, but now since I know a lot of folks, I find it a surprising source of enlightenment and literary inspiration. It also helps that Red Jergens has been a good friend to me when it comes to promoting my latest novels in the *Banner*.

I touch the icon on my phone for the Hoosier Lottery and nearly choke on my coffee when I see that the Whopper Ball is over $500 million. Stella approaches my table with my lunch platter and sees me looking at the lottery number. "Are you gonna pick up some tickets, Nathan? If you win, you know you have to share some with me!"

"Of course I would, Stella, but you know that the chances of winning are like one out of 300 million, right? I've never understood why someone would spend their hard-earned money just to throw it away on a fool's dream."

Now, truth be known, I find Stella to be an intriguing woman. First of all, despite being in her midfifties she's kept herself looking very nice. She's about 5'5" tall and has lustrous honey blond hair that cascades down her shoulders like a mare's mane. Her face is pretty and despite the few extra pounds that most of us carry, she's got a cute figure and dresses nicely. But, what I find the most attractive about Stella is that she's smart as a whip and knows most of the gossip that goes on in our community. I mean, just like some bartenders are good listeners and "therapists" for their regular patrons, a lot people just feel comfortable sharing their pain and hopes and dreams with Stella. She's seen and heard it all.

I take my sweet time enjoying my sandwich and fries, and before long, I'm nearly the last person in the diner. "More coffee?" Stella asks. "We've got some peach cobbler if you've got any room left."

"No, thank you, I'm pretty full, but I will take another cup of coffee if you've got time to join me."

"Let me take care of these last folks, and we can sit a spell and visit." She sashays off, and five minutes later it's just me and her with two cups of fresh, full-bodied coffee.

"So, what have you been up to?" I ask Stella. "Aside from feeding the good people of Putnam County."

"That's about it really. The good news is that I have a thriving business. The bad news is that I don't have much of a life outside of the diner. Don't get me wrong, Nathan, I love it here, and it seems that a lot of other folks do too. So …"

"Well, it sure seems like you've got your finger on the pulse of the comings and goings in our community."

"Yeah, I'm surprised by how many people want to share very personal affairs with me, and yeah, sometimes that does include romantic affairs, but in the main some, folks just feel comfortable telling me what's on their minds which I respect and keep confidential."

"You're a good woman, Stella."

"So, what're you working on these days, Nathan? Got another literary gem in the making?"

"Well, thanks for calling them gems. Sure wish my sales reflected that, but it is what it is, and I just love writing despite my modest commercial success. Frankly, I write for my own personal entertainment and if other people enjoy my books, then that's a happy bonus."

"But, you're working on a new novel, right?"

"Yeah, I am, but for some reason I'm not totally connected with the story I'm telling. I've been tinkering with another sequel in the Engel Family series, but I just don't feel fully motivated to go beyond *The Write House* and *Kindred Spirits*. I mean, local folks like the stories because they're set here in Greencastle, but I keep thinking there's a fresh, new direction that's calling out to me. Anyway, I imagine it'll come sooner or later."

We chat for a few minutes longer and then Stella looks at her watch and says, "I've got to get busy again, Nathan. I'm short a cook today so that means I'm pulling double duty."

"Yeah, I'll get out of your hair and let you go." I hand her a twenty dollar bill and then put another twenty on the table as I get up.

"Thanks! Where you heading now?" she asks.

"Oh, I gotta stop at the grocery store. With Marlita and her sisters leaving the country on Tuesday, I need to stock up on some things. Then, I'll see if she needs me to help her get ready for her grand adventure. I doubt that she will, but I think I get brownie points for at least offering to help."

Stella and I give each other a parting wave, and I exit the Monon and climb back into Pappy. I stare at the exterior of the building and find that it's got a lot of charm, much of it exuded from within, I muse.

"Very fine woman," I think to myself. "Someone who can probably be trusted to protect personal secrets."

I turn right out of the diner's parking lot and head toward the center of town. I hear the courthouse bell ring twice and smile thinking of my last novel, *Kindred Spirits,* in which a magical bell communicated its thoughts with my heroine, Aurora. I know, the supernatural elements sound a little too "woo woo" for some people, but ever since I visited the Kennedy Bell Farm a few years ago, I knew I wanted to spin a yarn about spirited bells.

I turn east on Washington Street and cruise past the community foundation's office building, my bank, and my dentist's office. Three minutes later I arrive at Barney's grocery store and guide Pappy into a parking spot. As usual, I sit in my truck for a minute watching people come and go with their shopping carts. I never know when a creative thought will occur to me and sometimes watching folks in their daily lives often strikes me with some unexpected inspiration. I know, it sounds weird, but it works...well sometimes.

I exit my truck and head inside, grab a cart, and politely wait for an elderly woman to make her way in front of me. With Marlita teaching a thriving yoga practice and handling a ton of other family obligations, I've taken over the duty of purchasing about 90 percent of our groceries. Truth is, it's kinda entertaining. While I wouldn't exactly call going to Barney's a social event, you never know who you'll run into, especially in the produce section.

I reach inside my shirt pocket and find my wadded-up grocery list: Avocados, berries, nuts, a healthy variety of fresh veggies and fruit, cheese, bread, laundry detergent, and a nice bottle of wine for Marlita.

"Hello, Nathan!" I hear a cheerful voice sing out to me. "Loved reading *The Write House!*"

I have no idea who this lady is, but regardless, anyone who says they love my books is an instant friend. "Thank you very much," I reply. "And, stay tuned because I'm working on another suspense story, and it's set here in Greencastle too!" My new friend beams at me, and my writer's ego swells to the size of a Buick.

As I wander down the aisles, I'm taken by how many foods just aren't very healthy for us. Things loaded with sugar and carbs, not to mention processed meats and Cheese Whiz, whatever the heck Cheese Whiz is! I look at my grocery list to make certain that I've gotten everything I need for now and navigate my way to the self-checkout scanner. As I approach I see an employee named Marianne standing by the information counter. I can't help but notice that the Whopper Ball lottery is up past $500 million. On a lark I say, "Oh, screw it!" and against my better judgment, I purchase a ticket from Marianne.

"You know, Mr. Andrews, if you win you have to share some money with me!"

"I can't believe I'm wasting my money on a stupid lottery ticket, but I'll definitely give you something if I win." I stuff the ticket in my pocket, pay for my groceries, and amble back to Pappy. The drive home is uneventful, but I continue to fret about the direction of my new novel.

"Damn! Try as I might, this story just isn't working for me."

I carefully pull into our driveway which is full of cars belonging to Marlita's yoga students and park in our carport. I turn Pappy's engine off and just sit there staring in the distance.

What the heck am I going to do about this book? I don't relish the thought of starting all over again on a fresh story, but the thought of forcing a story to unfold isn't something I welcome either. Writer's block, I wonder. I don't think so. I've always believed that a story either flows or it doesn't. I shrug off the dilemma, exit Pappy with my groceries, and saunter inside…still wondering.

Chapter Three

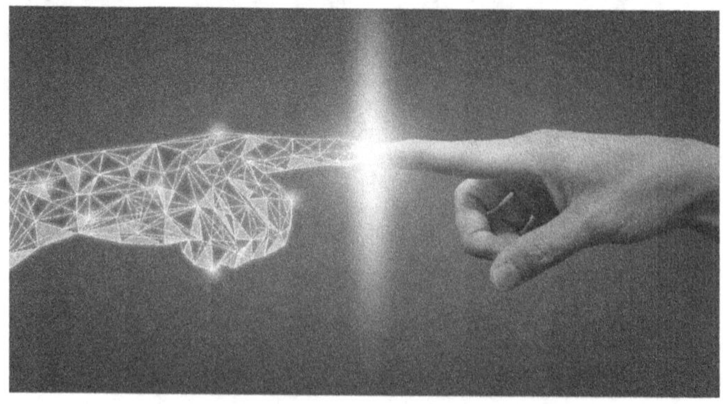

THE NEXT COUPLE OF DAYS pass rather quickly. Marlita has been like a whirling dervish doing laundry and trying to decide what to pack for a three-week trip. She and her sissies always try to pack their belongings to carry on board so they don't have to worry about their bags getting lost in transit. Easier said than done. Finally, it's Monday evening, and the Stanley sisters have decided to spend the night in a motel near the Indianapolis airport so they can easily catch a very early flight the next morning.

"Now, you promised me you'd try to eat healthy meals while I'm gone, right Nathan? I left you plenty of nutritious food in the freezer."

"Yes, darling, you can count on me!"

She gives me a skeptical look and a big hug. "I don't know what our internet service will be like in some of the places we're staying, but I promise to contact you as often as I can."

"I know you will. Don't worry about me. Just be safe and have a terrific time. Bella and I will take care of home and hearth while you're gone."

Marlita gives me a warm hug and kisses me sweetly. "I love you, Nathan Andrews! To the moon and back!"

"Me too, sweetie," I reply a little wistfully. "I'll miss you bunches." We kiss again, and then she's out the door.

The next morning I wake to a bell tone on my phone. It's a text from Marlita letting me know that she, BJ, and Linda are about to board their flight to Paris and then on to Athens. *Bon voyage!* I text back. *Safe travels! I love you!* I lie in bed a few more minutes longer trying to fall back asleep, but Bella leaps on the bed as if to announce that's it's time for me to get up and moving. Reluctantly, I obey and waddle downstairs to the kitchen to start the coffee pot. I catch a glimpse of my reflection in the window and smile thinking about how Marlita and I often show up for breakfast with our hair in total disarray.

"Well, you're just a mess, Nathan Andrews!" Marlita likes to tease me when I look like this. Truth is, I am a mess, but whatever, right?!

After a simple breakfast of coffee with toast, peanut butter, and blueberries, I dutifully go about doing my morning chores: Washing a few dishes, making the bed, emptying ashes from our wood furnace, hauling a load of firewood into the basement, taking yesterday's salad greens out to our chickens, and making sure that Bella has plenty of food and fresh water. Those chores take me about thirty minutes, and then I wonder what the heck to do with the next umpteen hours of the day.

I climb the stairs up to the sanctity of my office, turn on my computer, and open the novel that I've been working on. I honestly feel like I've written some very good passages, but I still remain flummoxed about where I want to go with the story. So, I end up staring absently into space and putzing around with things on my desk. I notice the lottery ticket I'd purchased at the grocery store a few days ago and see that the drawing was last night. I click on the Hoosier Lottery icon on my computer and follow the prompt to scan my ticket.

What I see next on my computer screen has me even more flummoxed than the novel I've been trying to write.

You have a winning ticket! You've won the Whopper Ball Jackpot!

"What the hell!" I blurt out loud. "This has got to be a bad joke!"

I stare at my computer screen for what seems like an eternity, and check the numbers on my lottery ticket against the winning numbers on the screen. Son-of-a-bitch if they don't match. I check the winning amount, and it reads $514 million.

"Holy crap! There's no way this is possible." I continue to stare at my computer in rapt disbelief. I get up from my desk and wander into the bathroom. I splash water on my face and stare at my reflection in the mirror. I'm the same guy with disheveled hair, only now I'm sporting a wet, bewildered expression. "There's no way this is legit!" I murmur out loud. "No freaking way!"

I decide to shave and shower thinking that when I look at my computer afterward that the real world will have regained its sanity. Fifteen minutes later I've finished up in the bathroom and gotten dressed. I cautiously peek inside my office half expecting to see a weird portal to another realm, but it's my same old office. My computer has gone into sleep mode, and I click the return key to bring it back to life. The Hoosier Lottery website immediately reappears showing the same stunning results of the Whopper Ball drawing. $514 million. I plop down in my chair and just stare vacantly as if I'd been hit by lightning.

I begin to call out to Marlita so she can confirm what I'm seeing but quickly remember that she's already a continent away. "Holy guacamole! What do I do now? Who do I call to see if this is real?"

To say that I'm perplexed is the understatement of a lifetime. I've always read that if you ever win the lottery you should place the ticket in a very secure place and then contact an attorney and accountant for legal advice and financial planning. I imagine there are other things a winner should immediately do, too, like sign the back of the ticket, but just in case, I choose not to do that until I speak with a lawyer. I turn on my printer and make a few copies of the ticket and place it in the safe in my office where I keep other important papers like my will and the deed to the house. And then I do what any self-respecting, mature adult would do under these circumstances, I begin laughing uncontrollably and dancing around like someone's lit my underwear on fire. "Woohooooo!!!"

Once I calm down, I say to myself, "I need to call Joe." Joseph Daniels is our family's estate attorney in Cincinnati. I've known him for many years and really trust his lawyerly acumen mainly because he's really smart, and he has a very good heart. Joe went to Harvard for his undergraduate degree, then got his law degree at the University of Virginia. After that he began his career at Hoffman, Fabian and True, a venerable law firm in Cincinnati, where he specializes in estate planning and philanthropy. "Yeah, Joe's the right guy to call."

I go to the contacts on my phone and press his phone number. It rings a few times, and then I hear Joe's familiar voice say, "Nathan, how are you? I've been meaning to call you. I finished your most current novel last week and really enjoyed it. I don't know how you keep coming up with these great stories, but I'm really impressed."

"G'morning, Joe, and thanks! I hope I'm not calling you too early, but I have something really important I need to discuss with you."

"Never too early for you, old friend. I went Of Counsel with the firm at the end of the year and happily spend more time working from my home office instead of trudging my way downtown. How's Marlita doing?"

"Marlita's doing fine, in fact she and her two sisters left earlier today for three weeks in Greece and Croatia, so it's just me and the cat holding down the fort here."

"So, what's up? How can I be of service?"

"Well, it's the damnedest thing, but I think I may've just come into a significant sum of money, and I need your expertise."

"Oh?! Like how significant?"

"Like so significant that I'd really rather speak with you in person than over the phone. Any chance I can get with you soon either in Cincinnati or preferably for you to come here to the farm? If I'm correct about the money, I'll be happy to make it worth your while beyond your usual fee."

"You're serious about this, aren't you?"

"Yeah, I am."

"Okay, hold on a sec while I check my calendar."

I hear Joe humming to himself while he looks at his schedule. "Sure, I think I can move a few meetings around, plus it'll feel good to get away from the big city and hang out in the country with a good friend. How about I come to your place around noon tomorrow?"

"Sounds great. The guest room is waiting for you, and I'll introduce you to the exciting cuisine at the Monon Diner."

"Do you want to give me a hint about your recent windfall or should I wait until tomorrow?"

"Let's wait till tomorrow, okay? I'm so stoked about this that I'm not sure how well I can contain my emotions right now."

"Wow, this does sound serious. You've certainly aroused my curiosity. Can't wait to get the full picture from you. Until tomorrow then, Nathan. See you around noon."

"Great…and thanks, Joe. You're a prince! I know you're a very busy guy, and I promise to make this trip worth your while."

Chapter Four

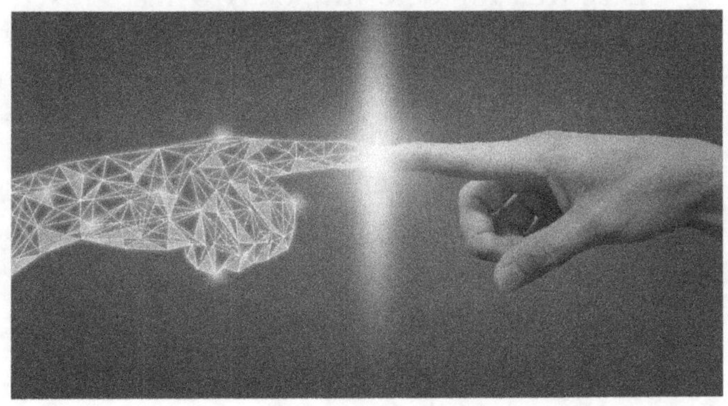

A FEW MINUTES BEFORE HIGH NOON the next day, I hear the sound of tires on our gravel driveway and see Joe Daniels arrive in his silver Audi. I watch as he exits his shiny ride and stretch his legs and back from his three-hour drive to Putnam County. I greet him at the back door and take his overnight bag inside which Bella immediately begins to sniff.

"How was your drive?"

"It was fine except for some late morning traffic on I-465 around Indy. Not bad though."

"C'mon in. I made some lunch for us, and then I want to show you something upstairs in my office."

During lunch Joe tells me about a few of the charitable boards of directors that he's serving on. "I swear I keep promising myself that I'm gonna cut back on my philanthropic work, but I just can't seem to say no."

"Well, those organizations are darn lucky to have you, Joe."

"You're kind to say so, Nathan. I wish my partners at the firm were as generous with their praise. It seems that all they think about is billable hours, and I don't bill those charities anything for legal work unless I ask another attorney to research something obscure."

We finish lunch, and I clean up a few dishes while Joe puts some belongings in the guest bathroom and grabs his briefcase.

"Let's head upstairs and prepare yourself for something a little mind boggling. At least, I hope it boggles your brain since I hauled you all the way out here."

We enter my cozy office, and I pull another chair up to my desk so we can view my computer screen together. I retrieve the Whopper Ball lottery ticket from my safe and lay it face down while I bring up the Hoosier Lottery website.

"Are you ready for this?" I ask Joe who has a confused expression on his face. Then, I turn the ticket over, and he looks at the ticket and then at the lottery website, then at the ticket again.

As I mentioned earlier, Joe is a very bright guy, and he understands legal verbiage as well as anyone, but at this moment all of his proper training and legal lingo disappear, and he blurts out, "You've got to be shittin' me!"

I look at him. He looks at me, and we both begin laughing our asses off.

"Now seriously, Joe, am I correct in believing that I just won the Whopper Ball jackpot?! I mean, like to the tune of $514 million?!"

Joe carefully checks the numbers on the ticket against the numbers shown on the website, and he soberly replies, "It would appear that you have!" He looks at the ticket and the computer screen again and nods his head affirmatively. "Sure as hell looks like it, Nathan! Unbelievable, my friend! Or, should I say, my very wealthy friend!"

I pull a dollar bill out of my pocket and ask him: "Would you consider this modest dollar as a down payment on a retainer for your legal services going forward?"

"Yeah, I think we can work something out," he laughs, "But only if you also agree to treat me to dinner tonight."

"Yeah, I think we can work something out," I repeat, "But first please tell me what my strategy should be for redeeming the ticket and how to proceed."

Over the next hour or so Joe does some calculations for various tax treatments and the benefits of taking a direct cash payout versus an annuity over 29 years. Here's the rub of what he said: "First of all you have 180 days before you have to present your ticket to the lottery commission, so we don't have to make any immediate decisions other than to keep the ticket very safe."

"What about my signing the back of it? I've always heard it's recommended that the winner do that."

"Great question. It all comes down to a matter of your personal privacy and security. Some winners get so excited that they shout their success out to the entire world, and that only welcomes tons of people showing up on your doorstep asking for a handout. Granted, in many cases those asking for money represent legitimate charitable organizations, but trust me, every long-lost relative and anyone with a clever business scheme will also hound you."

"So, what do you suggest?"

"My inclination is for you *not* to sign the back of the ticket, but instead I recommend that you deposit your winnings into a trust that does not require your name and thereby ensures your privacy. We should create the trust prior to going to the lottery commission. I could serve as trustee, but only you, Nathan Andrews, would have power over the money, like signing checks or making transfers, etc. No one else unless you direct otherwise."

"What about taking the annuity payments spread over twenty-nine years versus the direct cash payout?"

"Yeah, there's no question you'll leave a lot of money on the table if you take the direct cash payout versus the annuity. In fact, you'll receive only about 52 percent of the winning amount."

I grab my calculator and figure 52 percent of $514 million. "That reduces it to over $267.2 million."

"Close enough, but remember you have to pay federal tax, and Indiana state income tax, too which reduces your winnings by about another $120,000. But, you're still looking at a stunning windfall around $267 million. Do you think you could live off of that?"

"Uh yeah, I think I might be able to squeak by with only that. So, what else do you recommend, Joe?"

"We can also reduce your tax liability by creating a separate charitable trust so you can make distributions to 501(c) (3) organizations, and it would probably be wise to deposit the money among a couple of banks, like maybe a bank in Indianapolis, one in Cincinnati, and another in Chicago. All of those deposits would be in the name of the trust, again to maintain your anonymity. You should also consider retaining an astute accountant and a money manager in addition to my legal oversight. These are all things that we have time to arrange before going to the lottery commission."

"What else?" I ask.

"Winning this amount of dough is going to change your life, Nathan. I suggest you tell no one about this except Marlita, and she should be encouraged to exercise absolute secrecy, even with her sisters and her son, Christopher, at least in the short-term."

I nod my understanding. "I don't think I want to even share this news with her until she returns from Europe. I'm not sure how much I trust the security of international texting or emails."

"Good point, Nathan, plus we still need to confirm that you have, indeed won the entire Whopper Ball jackpot, and that there are no other people with winning numbers. Regardless, you're still gonna come into a boatload of cash."

"I hadn't even thought about that."

"Other things for you to consider are not spending a dime on any really major purchases or gifts for at least three months so you don't signal to the world that you've got a ton of dough. You and Marlita may even wish to consider moving away from Greencastle and have your mail go to a P.O. box."

"Seriously?"

"It's something to think about. I can recommend a trustworthy accountant for you if you wish and a low-fee money manager with a reputable investment firm. You'd be surprised by the number of jackpot winners that go broke within five years because they didn't plan well."

I nod my head in understanding.

"Why don't I take an hour or so here in your office and crunch some more numbers for you and do a little more research into best strategies for lottery winners and the creation of trusts. I'll head back to Cincinnati in the morning and can begin preparing some documents for you to review."

Again, I nod my understanding. "Thanks, Joe, I really appreciate your taking me on as a client. When we finally have a pretty good idea of how much I'll receive, I hope you know I'll be happy to sweeten your usual fee."

"Thanks, Nathan! That's something we can discuss later. For now, let me get started on some initial work, and then we can grab some of that great cuisine at the Monon Diner."

"This is very helpful, Joe. I definitely heard you when you advised me not to make any immediate major purchases or gifts, but while you're working on this, I think I'll go and fantasize about worthy people and charitable organizations that I might like to support."

"Any one immediately come to mind, or would you prefer not to say yet?"

"Yeah, it's premature for me to name names quite yet, but I do believe that I have some, uh, unfinished business I'd like to tend to. I'll be downstairs. Give me a holler when you're ready to go to dinner."

About two hours later Joe joins me in the family room with a broad smile on his face. "This is pretty damn amazing, Nathan. I mean, I've dealt with some very high net worth individuals and families in my practice, but your situation ranks right up there with them, if not more."

"You know, I've never really envied superrich people. Even when I was doing charitable fundraising in Cincinnati, I worked with a lot of wealthy donors and folks on our boards of directors, but I always viewed their dough as fuel for the machinery to do good things like build hospital wings at Children's Hospital or improve interpretive exhibits at the zoo. That's what always impressed me the most."

"Yeah, I get it. Now, you'll have an opportunity to craft your own legacy of giving, and that's a beautiful thing."

"True, but you know what I really want to do first?!" I ask enthusiastically.

"What's that?"

"Eat! C'mon let's go to the Monon for some down-home cookin'. And, I want you to meet the owner, Stella."

We grab our jackets, exit the house without even locking the door, and climb into Pappy.

"Think you'll buy a new vehicle?" Joe asks.

"Maybe, but I'll always keep Pappy. I'm just a simple country feller after all."

Twelve minutes later we arrive at the Monon Diner, and again I see Joe sportin' a broad grin on his face. "Not exactly the Maisonette or Pigall's restaurant, Nathan."

"No, I guess not, but the food's great and a helluva lot cheaper!"

I lead the way inside, and we're immediately greeted by Stella who gives me a warm hug. "And who's this dashing-looking fella?" she asks as she sizes Joe up.

"Stella, this is my good friend, Joe Daniels. Joe, this is Stella Chastain!"

"Bonjour, mademoiselle!" Joe croons. "It's a pleasure to meet you! Nathan has told me about your fine establishment, but I had no idea that the owner would be so lovely!" He bends forward and lightly kisses her hand.

Stella blushes like a rose in bloom. "Oh my, Nathan, where did you ever find such a refined gentleman?"

"Joe and I go way back to my Cincinnati days. We're good friends, but he's also my attorney. Got a table for two hungry gents?"

Stella can barely keep her eyes off Joe, nor can half of the women in the diner who saw him kiss her hand. "Uh, right this way, fellas, I've got a special table for you."

We get settled at the table, and Stella takes our drink orders then hustles away to the bar.

"Interesting place, Nathan." He nods toward Stella and says, "I see why you enjoy coming here."

"Yeah, Stella's great, but I'm a one-woman sort of guy, and I've got my hands full just trying to keep up with Marlita. But hey, knock yourself out. Stella's single, and I imagine she looks pretty good naked."

"So, what do you recommend for dinner, Nathan?"

"I'm partial to the steaks and fried chicken, but I suggest that you stay away from the chicken-fried steak. I ordered it once and teased Stella that I could still see the marks where the jockey was hittin' it!"

Stella brings our drinks, and we both order ribeyes and then spend the next hour or so catching up on the Cincinnati scene, his law practice, and my novels.

"Do you miss Cincinnati at all?" he asks.

"No," I reply without hesitation. "I mean, I miss some people, but in the main I'm very happy living in the country with Marlita. Plus, I don't have to deal with traffic and bosses."

"Well, from what I can tell, you've got a very good life. The country and small town livin' seem to suit you quite well, Nathan."

We finish our dinners, and I suggest that we head back home and enjoy a few nightcaps on the porch before calling it a night. Joe bids Stella a fond adieu with light kisses on both of her cheeks. "Until we meet again, dear lady," he whispers.

Stella nearly melts, and I give her a friendly wink. Joe and I strut out of the Monon like a couple of aging sex symbols and climb back into Pappy. The drive back home is lighthearted. Nothing like winning the lottery and eating a filling dinner at the Monon to put a smile on one's face.

We arrive home several minutes later, and I feed Bella and give her some attention while Joe checks his messages and texts a client and one of his partners. We go outside onto the front porch and listen to the night's sounds. The peepers are actively croaking at our pond and crickets are chirping to their potential mates. Spring is definitely here, and it feels like a rebirth of my world.

After drinking a half-bottle of Four Roses bourbon and getting the lowdown on people I used to know in Cincinnati, we finally call it a night. I make certain Joe has what he needs in the guest room, and I saunter upstairs three-sheets-to-the-wind! Before climbing into bed, I go into my office and send a mushy text to Marlita. Warily, I take one final peek at the Hoosier Lottery website to make sure this hasn't all been a dream. I see a few handwritten notes on my desk that Joe made earlier while researching my winnings. I'm very glad he joined me on the farm, and that I have someone I trust to share this wildly incredible happenstance.

That night I sleep fitfully, dreaming about a large sum of money that's miraculously come my way. Images of people I've known flit about me, mostly with good memories, but others bring troubling thoughts of things I could've, should've handled better. Unfinished business that I've suppressed for a long time. Somewhere in my dreams I hear the

peepers and crickets again. Yes, springtime is here…
a time of rebirth, a renaissance, an opportunity for
Nathan Andrews to show more character. The next
morning I awake, both refreshed and disconcerted.

"Man, hang on tight, Nathan!" I murmur to
myself. "Life is about to get very interesting!"

Chapter Five

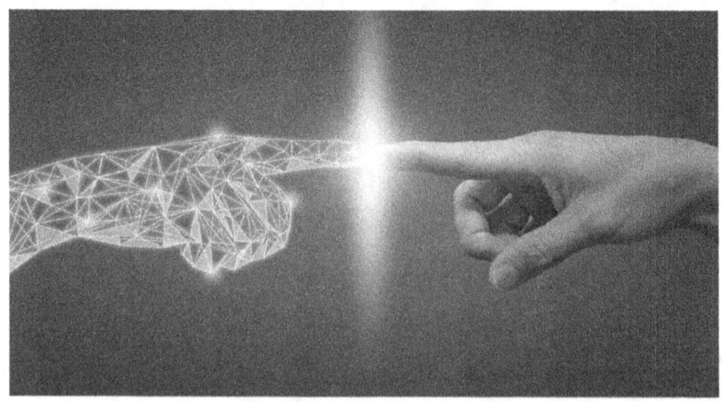

WANDER DOWNSTAIRS to the kitchen around eight o'clock and see Joe fully dressed, drinking coffee, and poring over notes and figures on his laptop. "G'morning, Nathan, how'd you sleep last night?"

"Pretty well with the exception of a few weird dreams. What're you working on?"

"Oh, I've got this writer as a client who lives in the middle of the freakin' Indiana who just became a gazillionaire," he laughs. "The dude gave me a whopping dollar bill as a retainer, so I'm hard at work trying to earn my keep and prepare some documents for him to review."

"Cool! Anyone I know?"

Joe ignores my superfluous question and turns his laptop so I can see his notes. "Seems like the initial tax calculations I did yesterday are fairly accurate. Without giving him your name, I'd like to have the senior tax attorney with our firm go over my figures to see what he thinks."

"Sounds fine to me, Joe, anything else you need from me?"

"Not at this point. I've got your social security number, and the original of your will is in our vault. I want to review it again because I imagine we'll have to rewrite it after we confirm your winnings with the lottery commission. At some point I'll probably need to have copies of, say, three years of your tax returns, too, but we can wait."

I nod my understanding. "I still haven't told Marlita yet. Thought it might be a nice surprise for her when she returns home."

"Oh, she'll be surprised all right! I should have a good draft of a trust for you to review by the time she gets back. I'll also draft the articles of a separate charitable trust that can significantly reduce your tax exposure. I'm thinking that you fund the charitable trust with perhaps 25 percent of your winnings to use for grants to qualified charities that you respect, and you'd still have about $200 million in 'mad money' to spend on whatever you wish including gifts to family members and other individuals you'd like to help."

"Sure, have at it, Joe! I can already think of a few local charities that I'd like to support. Wow, this is gonna be really big stuff, isn't it? Like an opportunity to change lives, hopefully all for the better."

"Indeed, it is, Nathan! And, I'm delighted to have an opportunity to work with you on this."

We have some more coffee, and I prepare a healthy breakfast for us...our farm fresh eggs, berries, and wheat toast. We idly chat about nothing in particular, but Joe does comment about how much fun it was grazing at the Monon and gazing at Stella. Afterward, Joe packs his gear, takes a leak, and says he needs to hit the road.

"I'll get back to you soon, Nathan. I'm sure you've got a lot to think about. Who knows, maybe there's even a fresh, new novel in this for you. After all, truth is often stranger than fiction."

"I like that idea, Joe. I like it a lot! I've been waiting for an epiphany, and I think you've maybe hit upon it."

Bella and I walk Joe to the back door and say goodbye. He's one of the very few people left in Cincinnati that I still communicate with, and I feel a little wistful knowing that the city where I spent decades living and building a career is now a distant memory. He honks his horn and waves as he pulls out of our driveway. I watch his silver Audi travel down our county road until it's out of sight, and I'm alone again with my cat and a world of wonders to explore.

Bella keeps me company while I putz around in the kitchen. As I wash the dishes, I look out the window and view our barnyard and the land beyond. We have a lovely home and property, and I sure can't imagine Marlita ever wanting to leave here. Me neither, but knowing that we can afford to go anywhere we want gives me pause about owning another house in a warmer clime that we can visit, especially in the depths of winter. All things Marlita and I can have fun pondering.

I climb the steps toward my office, and Bella races past me as if we're playing a game. Once there, I gently swoosh her off my desk chair and sit down at my computer. I log on and see an email from Marlita. She and her sissies have arrived safely on the Greek island of Hydra, and she sends me bunches of love and reminds me to eat healthily. I reply with yet another mushy email, but choose not to tell her about the Whopper Ball jackpot and Joe's visit. It feels like it would be premature to do so, and I prefer not to distract her from their grand adventure. I reckon she'll learn all about it soon enough. After sending my reply to her, I take a brief look at the manuscript that I've been struggling with and save it to an external hard drive.

"I'm done with you for now," I declare out loud. Perhaps there's another sequel to my Engel Family saga still waiting to be written, but for now I'm beginning to think of an exciting new direction. Joe's suggestion about using my lottery winnings as the focus of an entirely new story is something that's resonating with me. Now, I just need to figure out the who, what, where, why, when, and how. I smile at that thought and begin considering which organizations and people I might like to help financially. During my fundraising career, I remember a wealthy board member at Children's Hospital once telling me that it's harder to give money away well than it is to raise it. I guess I'm about to find out.

I keep myself somewhat busy over the next few days which is a glorified way of saying that I do a couple of daily chores but make sure I have ample time for naps and watching YouTube videos. I've particularly enjoyed just driving around town, now viewing civic and cultural organizations that I'm familiar with in a totally different way: Our great library and museum, the homeless shelter and animal shelter, Asbury Chapel which is the home to our world-famous Greencastle Summer Music Festival, the visitors bureau and park board, and our community foundation. They're all organizations that I respect.

One of the things that I'll have to decide is how to ensure Marlita's and my anonymity. I mean, as much fun as it would be to drop by the library and lay a cool million dollar check on the director's desk, it wouldn't take long for every worthy cause to camp out on our doorstep. Then, too, there are the potential crazies that might get aggressive. So, Joe's advice about not making any major purchases or gifts for at least three months makes a ton of sense. We sure don't want to draw a lot of attention to ourselves. I just need to be smart about this and probably identify some people I trust to serve as "agents," for a lack of a better term, to help me safely make gifts to both charitable organizations and deserving people in need. I'm starting to grasp what that trustee at Children's Hospital meant about the challenge of giving away money wisely.

Then, I start pondering which people I might like to help in a major way, some here in Greencastle and some in Cincinnati. A few names immediately come to mind, a couple because they're deserving and one or two out of guilt. And, of course, I realize that once I tell Marlita about our new-found wealth, I want her to feel free to select her own beneficiaries. I chuckle to myself when I think of an old W.C. Fields line: *"Money's like manure. It's not any good unless you spread it around."* I'm actually the second person to admit that I have a rather quirky sense of humor. Marlita's the first!

Over the next ten days, I find myself enjoying a lot of meals at the Monon Diner mainly because I enjoy the food, but because I've taken an interest in the way that Stella communicates with her customers. It's not like I purposefully eavesdrop on their conversations, but it's clear to me that people just seem to gravitate to her and share intimate details about their lives. Stella's a very good listener, and I find it curious how diverse her customers are. Some appear to be well-off financially while others seem down on their luck and needing a helping hand. I admire that Stella treats them all with the same respect. I tuck this notion away in my brain thinking that she could very well have a handle on folks whose lives I might be able to help.

So, three weeks have now come and gone since Marlita left for Greece and Croatia with her sisters, and I finally hear her Subaru pull into our carport. I dash outside to welcome her home and help with her luggage.

"There you are! You're finally back home. Can't wait to hear about your adventures."

She gives me a warm hug and a wet smooch. "Oh my God, Nathan, we had such a good time! I'll tell you all about it, but first I really need to pee." She leaves me in the driveway and goes dashing past Bella. Three minutes later she meets me and the cat in the kitchen with a huge smile.

"I don't even know where to begin. The scenery was awesome, our accommodations were mostly excellent, and the food and wine were terrific. The three of us joked about doing our laundry and flying back tomorrow. It was that much fun! Sorry, our internet service wasn't always the best so it was hard to send messages to you as often as I'd liked."

"Oh, I get it. Internet can still be iffy in a lot of remote places. I'm just thrilled that you, BJ, and Linda had such a great time and that you're home safe and sound! I missed you."

"Me too. But, what about you? Anything really interesting happen while I was gone?"

"Anything really interesting? Uh, yeah, but let's get you settled first. I'm sure you're exhausted and have a ton of things to catch up on. Tomorrow morning will be soon enough, okay?"

Marlita gives me a quizzical look. "Okay, but I bet it's about your new book, isn't it?"

"In a manner of speaking. I have something to show you tomorrow morning, and that's all I want to say right now…"

Chapter Six

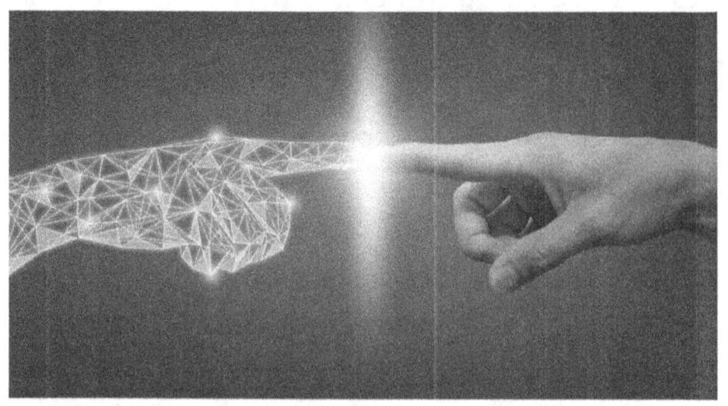

THE NEXT MORNING I WAKE UP EARLY and quietly go into my office to consider possible directions for a new story while Marlita slumbers away and fills the bedroom with the dulcet sounds of snorts and snores. I sometimes wonder how it's possible for such a lovely woman to make such noises, and I won't even mention the endearing toots she makes when she eats too many peanuts. Ah! Love's a wonderful thing!

I'm deep in thought when Marlita sneaks up behind me and wraps her arms around my neck. "I knew you'd be in here, Nathan. What're you working on?"

"Oh, good morning, darling. I hope you slept well. It sure sounded like you were."

"I did sleep well. No matter how much I enjoy traveling especially with my 'sissy bitches,' it's always great to come home to you and sleep in our bed. So, what is it you said was 'really interesting' that happened while I was away?"

"Here," I say as I pull up another chair so we can sit at my desk together. I pull up the Hoosier Lottery website and say, "Take a look at this. The Whopper Ball listing still shows the jackpot at $514 million."

"Wow! I wonder if anyone won."

I get up from my chair and walk over to my safe that I've concealed in my office closet and pull out my winning ticket. I lay it on my desk, and Marlita casually looks at it.

"So, did you win six dollars like that time before?"

"Compare the numbers, smartypants!"

Marlita looks at the lottery ticket, then at the Whopper Ball listing, then at me. "Nathan, this isn't real, is it? I mean, seriously, is this for real?"

"Yes, it's for real, my love, and we're about to become very rich!"

"Does this mean we can finally buy new carpet for the upstairs?" she laughs.

"Hell, we could probably buy an entire North Carolina carpet mill if we want."

"Nathan, seriously, is this for real?"

"It is. I asked Joe Daniels to come here from Cincinnati while you were away, so he could verify the veracity of my winning ticket, which he did, and he's already drafting some documents for a trust in which to deposit the winnings and a separate trust for charitable contributions. Once I have the legal documents prepared and have retained the other professionals I want to use, then I'll go to the Indiana Lottery Commission to claim our dough."

Marlita has a stunned expression on her face. "How much could we get?"

I show her Joe's initial calculations. "If we take the direct cash payout, and after we pay the federal and state taxes, we should still have over $265 million, give or take a few million."

"Holy shit! Why didn't you tell me earlier?"

"Because I didn't trust the privacy of the internet, and well, I wanted to surprise you."

"Well, you surprised me all right. I can't wait to tell my sisters and Chris and Elizabeth!"

"We don't want to do that right away, honey. In fact, Joe has advised that we not whisper a word to anyone, including family members, until we make legal and financial plans. As hard as that will be for both of us, he's right. If word of this gets out prematurely, we might as well pack up and move away from Putnam County because we won't have a moment's peace from people, no matter how well intentioned they might be…and then there are the people who might not be so well-intentioned too."

She nods her understanding. "Whew!"

"Yeah, 'whew' is right! Joe's working out the legal stuff for us, and we'll have plenty of opportunity in the future to share some details with our family, but we have to be VERY smart about this. Do I have your promise on that?"

"Yeah, I see your point, Nathan. Of course, I promise."

"So, darling, aside from that little surprise and Joe's visit, it was pretty quiet around here while you were gone."

"I don't know how you're able to stay so calm about this lottery jackpot, Nathan. I mean, this is the stuff that dreams are made of."

"Well, I've had three weeks to let it sink in a bit, but I have a feeling I'll be as gobsmacked as you are now once we actually claim our winnings. To tell the truth, it's been very hard not to fantasize about what we might buy and which charitable organizations and people we might like to support. My plan is for you to have your own stash of money to spend and donate however you please."

"Thanks, Nathan, this is really exciting...and a little scary. And by the way, no one uses the word 'gobsmacked' except for a stuffy writer! Couldn't you just say 'bewildered' or 'astonished?'"

I dodge the question. "Joe has suggested that we consider transferring perhaps $60 million into a charitable trust that can be directed to organizations, and we can use the remaining $200 million for…whatever. The charitable trust will help reduce our tax exposure, and remember, too, if we invest all of our money wisely, we can expect to receive beaucoup bucks from dividends and interest every year. Plus, nothing says we have to spend it all in the first year. We have a lot of years ahead of us yet. We should pace ourselves!"

"So, how do we protect our privacy and give money away at the same time?" she asks.

"Well, my first inclination is to have Joe on retainer to deliver grants to charitable organizations from an anonymous donor, and I have someone in mind to help identify needy folks locally, and to serve as our agent in making monetary gifts. She wouldn't be the sole person doing that for us because I want us to give gifts to family members and anyone else we choose that hopefully won't blab it all over town."

"She? Who's this 'she' you're thinking of?"

"I hesitate to tell you quite yet because we still have a lot to prepare for, and you might be a little surprised by my selection, but I think she could be ideal. Besides, I haven't spoken with her about this, and she may not even want to do it."

"Well, as long as you're not going to go running off with this 'she,' I guess I'm comfortable waiting for you to tell me."

"Good, and the only females I'm running off with are you and Bella, and your sissies can come along too."

Marlita leans against me and sighs, "I guess our lives are about to change big time, huh?"

"Yeah, it's a wonderful opportunity for us, and just think about all of that beautiful carpeting you're finally gonna buy."

"Cool! I'm thinking olive green and orange shag!" she teases. And, she thinks I have a quirky sense of humor!

———

The next several days seem to fly by. Marlita is engrossed in teaching her yoga classes, both at her studio and also at Asbury College's Reflection Center. Namaste y'all! As for me, I've begun consolidating my thoughts for the new book, and when I'm not doing that or running to town for something, I try to look busy whenever Marlita's around. *Nature abhors a vacuum*, and Marlita's got a work ethic that just doesn't quit.

I sit at my desk making a list of people and organizations that I want us to support, and also try figuring out how I want to write a very personal yet entertaining novel that my readers will enjoy. A title flies into my head…*Given Names*. I like it but want to remain open to other possibilities too. My phone rings, and it's Joe Daniels on the line.

"Hey Nathan, it's Joe, do you have a few minutes?"

"For you?! Of course. I've been looking forward to hearing from you. So, what's the good word?!"

"Well, I've got good news for you, and then I've got great news for you. Without mentioning your and Marlita's names, I asked our senior tax partner at the firm to review a scenario of an Indiana resident winning a Whopper Ball jackpot worth $514 million, and he confirmed that my figures were very close to what he computed."

"Terrific! Is that the good news or the great news?"

"The great news is that I've prepared drafts of two trust documents that I'm ready to share with you and Marlita. If you have time in the next few days, I'd be happy to drive to Greencastle again and go over things with the two of you. Maybe even enjoy another dinner at the Monon Diner."

I look at my calendar and see that Wednesday looks good for both Marlita and me. "Yeah, with Asbury College on break, Marlita's free that day so that's good for us if it works for you."

"Looks open for me too. Great, I'll see you guys day after tomorrow then, say around five o'clock."

We chat just a moment longer, then Joe tells me he's gotta run. "My partners have been dogging me about billing more hours, so unless I hit the lottery jackpot too, I guess I've gotta keep slogging away."

"Well, Joe, we haven't discussed the details of your retainer yet, but if you agree to keep helping me out, I think I might be in a financial position to have you tell your partners to, uh, what's the politically incorrect term? Oh yeah…cram it!"

Chapter Seven

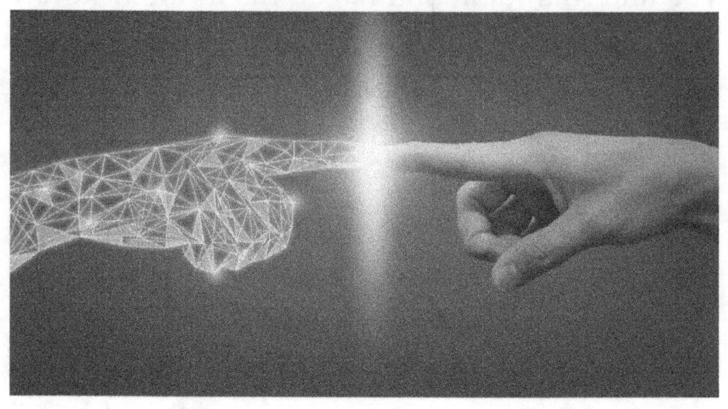

WEDNESDAY AFTERNOON COMES, and I hear Joe pull into our driveway a little before five o'clock.

"Marlita! How are you? It's been way too long. I hope you and your sisters had a great trip to Greece and Croatia."

She gives him a friendly hug. "Welcome, Joe! Yeah, we had a delightful trip, and I understand the two of you got into some, uh, lottery mischief while I was gone."

"We sure did! I mean, Nathan got into a little mischief. I'm just an innocent lawyer trying to help a buddy out."

I take Joe's overnight bag to the guest bedroom while Marlita prepares a late afternoon snack for us. We sit at the kitchen table, and the conversation gets serious.

"So, here are the drafts of the two trust documents that I've written for you. The first one is a charitable trust which I suggest you fund with approximately $60 million. I recommend that you use this trust to make grants to charitable organizations that you want to help. I would be honored to serve as the trustee for this trust, and like I told Nathan previously, only he would have power over the money, like signing checks, etc. I would be your 'agent,' as it were, to offer counsel and to follow your instructions. The second trust would be funded with the balance of your lottery winnings for you to use however you wish, i.e., gifts to family members and other noncharitable entities and people. Again, I'd be happy to serve as your trustee, and only Nathan would have power over the money. I'm in the process of rewriting Nathan's will so that in the event he predeceases you, Marlita, that you would be the decision-maker over all trust assets. Am I being clear, so far?"

"So far, so good, Joe," Marlita replies. "Where should we deposit the assets for the trusts?"

"My suggestion is that you divide the assets among three banks, perhaps in Indianapolis, Cincinnati, and Chicago, and probably some in your local Greencastle bank. There's no need to use your personal names for the trusts unless you choose to do so. This way we can maintain your anonymity. I also suggest that you select an excellent accountant or tax attorney to make certain everything is being done legally, and to prepare tax returns as needed. You're welcome to choose whomever you wish including Dave Greenbaum who heads the tax division at our law firm. I'm sure my law partners would be delighted to charge you for the billable hours, but this is entirely your choice."

"I'm comfortable with using him, Joe, if that's who you recommend."

"Well, he's excellent, and it would help streamline our oversight of your trust assets."

"That's fine," Marlita adds. "Let's use him."

"I also suggest that you choose a reputable money manager to invest much of your assets in safe, low-fee, dividend-paying securities."

"Sounds good, Joe, I think I'd like to ask Kyle Bartlett at Friedlander and Miller to be heavily involved. As you may recall F and M invested my parents' assets while they were alive, and I kept most of my dough with them until I moved to Indiana. Kyle's sharp, and I trust him."

"I know Kyle very well, and I agree he's a smart and trustworthy money manager. Anyway, I'd like you to talk about this, and then we can move forward. I'm sure each of the professionals we select will be thrilled to be involved."

"Gee, they might even be gobsmacked!" I chortle.

"Jeez, Nathan, enough with the 'gobsmacked' thing already," Marlita declares.

"Don't mind us, Joe. It's a private joke that Marlita doesn't find as amusing as I do!" She rolls her eyes.

"There's another very important thing that we need to discuss, Joe. How we make proper provisions for Brian's young children." Marlita grows very quiet at the mention of our deceased son's name, and I take her hand.

"Of course, you're right, Nathan. Forgive me, Marlita. I should've immediately thought of your providing for them. Such a tragic loss at such a young age. Let me get their full names and ages before I leave, and I can draft language to make certain they're generously cared for."

"Thank you, Joe," Marlita adds somberly. "I'll never get past his loss, but caring for the grandkids will help soften the blow a little."

"So, that's about it for now, I guess. Please take your time reviewing these drafts, and I can prepare the final trust articles for your signature, Nathan, as soon as you're ready."

"Then what?" I ask. "I actually feel very good about proceeding with everything you've outlined, Joe."

"Then, we open accounts with the banks to receive your assets and hire the tax attorney and money manager for their roles. After that, we'll be ready to go to the Lottery Commission in Indianapolis to claim your winnings."

"Wow, I can't believe this is really happening, Joe! Nathan told me that you advised him that we remain very tight-lipped about winning the lottery, and I'm comfortable with that."

"Excellent!" Joe replies. "It's in your best interests."

"One last thing, Joe, how much of a retainer will you require to serve as trustee for the trusts, and to assist with the grant-making to the charitable organizations?"

"I don't know for sure, Nathan. Since you're about to receive a ton of money, how about a million dollars?"

"How about four million?" I counter. "We want you totally committed and feeling appreciated!"

"Wow! Now, I'm feeling gobsmacked!" he effuses as Marlita smiles and rolls her eyes in feigned annoyance.

We decide to take a little break before heading off to the Monon Diner for dinner. Joe goes into the guest room to rest up a bit, and Marlita and I remain at the kitchen table to closely read the trust articles that Joe drafted. We're happy with what we see.

Thirty minutes later Joe emerges from the guest room and rejoins us. "I'm ready for dinner whenever you guys are."

"Why don't you two fellas go on without me?" Marlita suggests. "It's not really my type of food, and you can catch up some more."

"Are you sure?" I ask. "You know Stella will be happy to ask the kitchen to make whatever you want."

"I know, but I'm still full from our snack, and you gents can enjoy diner food while using words like gobsmacked to your hearts' content."

A few minutes more, and we're out the door. "Wanna take your Audi or Pappy?" I ask Joe.

"When in Rome…" Joe says, and we pile into Pappy.

We arrive at the Monon's parking lot around sevenish, and Joe is surprised that the lot's not crowded with dinner patrons.

"Ya gotta remember, Joe, this is Putnam County, Indiana. It's Wednesday night, and most people are either at home or have already eaten. Stella ordinarily closes the diner around eight because everyone's gone."

We enter the diner, and Stella greets us by the door. "Well, if it's not my favorite author and that handsome city feller again. Howdy, Nathan."

"Evening, Stella! You remember my good friend, Joe Daniels, don't ya?"

"Of course, I do. Great to see you again, Mr. Daniels. You sure caused quite a stir among the ladies the last time you were here showing off your charming citified manners."

I smile as I watch Joe bow and kiss Stella's hand again. "So good to see you again, Ms. Chastain. Your loveliness grows greater with each time I see you…and please call me Joe." Joe follows Stella's lead and walks over to an empty table.

Stella fawns excitedly. "Is he always this charming?" she whispers to me.

"I don't think so, Stella. I keep telling him you're the real deal, but I think he also finds you, uh, rather fascinating, and trust me, Joe Daniels could probably have his pick of any single woman in Cincinnati."

Stella gives us some time to check out the menu and returns a few minutes later to take our orders.

Joe and I talk quietly about the plans we discussed with Marlita, and I ask him if he'd be willing to personally hand-deliver grant checks to charities we select going forward. He gladly agrees.

"In addition to the grandchildren, what about other individuals you want to help? Have you thought about who you want to serve as your agent in those situations?"

"I have. Marlita and I want to personally give a bunch of money to Chris and Elizabeth, and perhaps a million dollars each to her sisters to begin with. I'm thinking there might be a few others I'd want to personally approach, too, but regarding other folks I have someone in mind who has her thumb on the pulse of deserving people in our community, and I wanted to get your opinion too."

"Oh?! Who?!"

I look in Stella's direction and nod toward her.

"Stella?" he asks with a surprised grin on his face.

"Think about it, Joe. I mean, she knows virtually everyone in the county. She's smart as a whip, and I believe she knows how to keep her secrets to herself. I think she could be an ideal person to hand-deliver checks to people, much the same way you'll do with the charities we pick. Moreover, I believe she would take her responsibility very seriously and help identify folks that are truly deserving."

Joe looks at me intently plumbing the depths of my sincerity. "You know, I think it's actually a brilliant idea. She's not someone I would've immediately thought of, but I believe you make a very compelling point, Nathan."

"Good, I was really hoping you'd feel that way. The diner's clearing out. Why don't we ask her to join us in a little conversation once everyone's gone?"

A few minutes later Stella says goodnight to the last dinner guests and flips the sign on the door to "closed." Stella tells the cook that he can call it a night which he gladly does.

"You fellas care for any dessert? We still have some yummy coconut cream pie left."

"No thanks," Joe and I say in unison, "but we'd appreciate it if you could join us. We have something we'd like to discuss with you."

"Oh? You didn't care for your dinner? Larry's a new cook. I thought everything looked okay."

"No, dinner was fine," Joe says. "Best walleye I've ever eaten."

I nod my agreement. "No, it's an entirely different matter. Actually, I have a *proposition* we'd like to discuss with you."

"Now look, fellas, all the hand kissin' and French words are a lot of fun and all, but I'm not sure what kind of proposition you're referring to. I just want to be clear that I'm not the kind of girl who fools around or gets involved in risky business ventures…It's just not who I am!" She starts to get up.

"I know that, Stella," I say soothingly. "I do have something very important I'd like to discuss with you, though, and perhaps 'proposition' was a poor choice of words. I meant no insult. Joe's here with me not only because we're friends, but he's also here in an official capacity as my attorney."

"Oh God, you're not going to sue me over some overcooked walleye are ya?"

Joe and I break out laughing. "No, the walleye was fine." I pause for a moment. "Before I go any further, though, I want you to tell me the honest truth about your willingness to keep a very important secret."

"Is your secret legal, or do I have to worry about losing my business and gettin' thrown in jail?"

"You have my word as an officer of the court that what we're about to ask you is not only totally legal, but it's also the opportunity of a lifetime."

"Well, that'll get a girl's attention!" She sits down next to Joe and our conversation begins.

"I'm about to come into a lot of money, Stella, and I was hoping you'd help me distribute some of it."

"Huh?!" Now she's the one laughing out loud. "Like what? Like giving a couple hundred bucks to the homeless shelter or the library? Heck, Nathan, that's something you can easily do. You don't need me for that."

"You're right, but what if I were in a position to give life-changing sums to people who are truly needy or deserving? I have a few people in mind, but I respect the knowledge you have about the people in our community. I guess I just have faith in your ability to use very good judgment. Make no mistake, however, I would always have the final say on who gets our support, but I wouldn't ask you to consider this if I didn't believe in you and would listen closely to your advice."

"You know, it all sounds good, but I'm a busy woman, what with running the diner and all. I wish I could help you guys out, and believe me I'm flattered as all get out, but I've got to make money to live and keep the Monon afloat."

"What if I were to offer you $3 million to help fund your livelihood, and for you to also help us with some life-changing philanthropy? Joe has agreed to serve as the trustee of my trusts and would be the lead person in giving grants to qualified charities. I want the two of you to help protect Marlita's and my anonymity while we give away a lot of dough. Joe would handle the majority of the charitable grants, and you would be my agent in helping some of our neighbors."

She stares at me with a look of total bewilderment. I'd use the word "gobsmacked" again, but even I know when enough is enough!

"Oh come on now. You're just toying with me."

"No, he's not, Stella. If you agree, I'll be happy to draft a contract stating your agreement in exchange for $3 million to be paid immediately upon our receiving our newly found money which should take about a month. This, dear lady, is totally legit, and I look forward to working with you on Nathan and Marlita's behalf."

"Our only condition," I add, "is that you maintain the strictest of secrecy as to who the money comes from. Marlita and I want to remain totally beneath the radar. If you were to violate that condition, you would forfeit the $3 million. Do we have an agreement?"

Stella looks at me, then at Joe, then at me again. "Yes, we do, Nathan, and I'm someone who knows how to keep a secret. I'm honored that you have such faith in me, and I promise never to let you down."

"Great! Joe'll send a contract next week for you to sign, plus a signing bonus to prove we're not just blowing smoke at you, okay?"

"Okay," she says thoughtfully. "And, thank you!"

Joe and I bid Stella a fond adieu and climb back into Pappy for the drive home.

"I think that went pretty well, Joe. What do you think?"

"I swear, Nathan Andrews, you're a man who's full of surprises."

We arrive home a few minutes later and share the news of Stella's agreement with Marlita and my rationale for choosing her.

"Seriously…Stella?!" She thinks about Stella's participation a bit longer and concurs, "Yeah, Stella could be ideal for all of the reasons you just explained, Nathan, and best of all, she's true blue, and no one would ever expect her of having access to great wealth."

Over the next several weeks, I see a lot of closure on the plans we'd discussed with Joe: I executed the trust agreements, and Joe signed on as trustee. We had our last will and testament updated. Joe sent the contract and a $100,000 signing bonus to Stella Chastain. We opened accounts at banks in Indianapolis, Cincinnati, and Chicago. We retained Dave Greenbaum at Hoffman, Fabian and True as our tax attorney and Kyle Bartlett at Friedlander and Miller as our main money manager. And finally, we drove to the Indiana Lottery Commission in Indianapolis and claimed my Whopper Ball lottery winnings totaling $267 million. Fortunately, I was the only person to win the entire jackpot, and my lovely Marlita and I are rich beyond words.

"It's a brave new world for us, darlin'! Now, we have to practice some degree of self control and let our consciences be our guide."

"So, how do you want to proceed, Nathan?"

"Great question, honey, and despite our both understanding Joe's advice not to spend a lot of money right away, I think we're both conservative enough in our spending habits that it's okay to make some initial gifts. If anyone asks, I can always fib and say my book sales have taken off. We both have a list of names of people and organizations that are dear to us. Would you like to select the very first one?"

"But, you won the money, Nathan. Why don't you go first?"

"Okay, how 'bout I select some people that we can both agree on?"

"Like?"

"Like Christopher and Elizabeth, your sisters, and Brian's children. Family comes first in my book, both literally and figuratively!"

And, that's what we did!

Chapter Eight

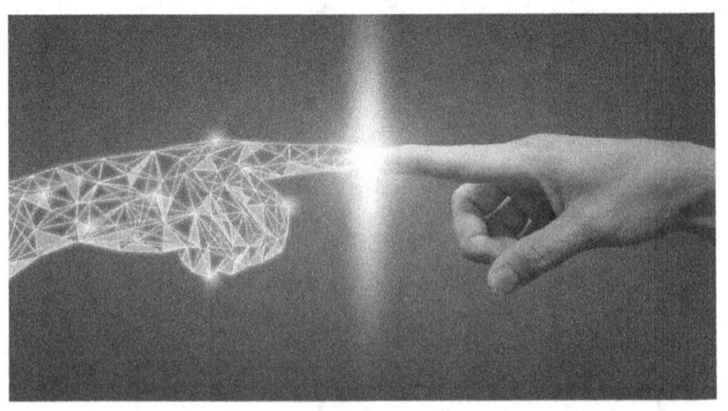

~ The Family ~

THE CONCEPT OF FAMILY is a very emotional subject for me mainly because when it comes to my nuclear family I feel like an orphan. My parents died over two decades ago, and my brother and I have been estranged for a long time thanks mainly to that mean-spirited shrew he's married to. I won't bore you with the details, but she came between my brother and me in ways that are still shocking and heartbreaking. Despite my estrangement from him, I'll always love him very much.

So, when Marlita and I came together nearly twenty years ago, I didn't quite know how to safely feel like a member of her family. Her parents were about as kind and loving as any people I've ever known, and watching them decline in their dotage and finally pass away was another heartbreaking loss that has healed somewhat over time but not fully. Alan and Donnabelle were that special. Alan was a devoted family man and an avid outdoorsman who loved to hunt and fish. Donnabelle was the quintessential wife and mother who always liked to ride in the country with her 'hubby' looking for deer and wild turkeys. I haven't discussed it with Marlita yet, but I plan on buying a large tract of woodland in Putnam County to create a nature preserve in their memories.

Marlita's sisters, BJ and Linda, are such a delight. It took me a few years to feel close to them, but I do, and my life is much richer because of them. Sadly, both of them lost their husbands, so in some ways our friendship has helped fill the void a little for each of us. Both of them are comfortable financially, not super rich by any means, but they don't have to worry about their next meals either. Regardless, I've decided that Marlita and I will give them each a million dollars at Christmas. Good luck on keeping that secret, huh?!

When it comes to Brian's children and his former wife, I totally defer to Marlita's recommendations. We've discussed the nature of our support a lot and listened closely to brother, Chris's, counsel too. The trust fund that Joe Daniels wrote makes ample resources available for the grandkids' education as far as they wish to go, and the children and their mother will never have to worry about living expenses, unless they go totally overboard, at which point I'm sure Marlita would, uh, *encourage* them to rein in their spending.

During his high school and college years, Brian was a star swimmer who attended IUPUI on a full-ride college scholarship and was captain of his team. He was a leader and inspiration to his teammates, and his natural leadership skills carried over into his career as a firefighter. Many of the swim meets he trained for and competed in were at the college's natatorium, and Marlita and I have thought seriously about approaching the college about naming rights in Brian's memory. I'm comfortable with these decisions which also help assuage some of my guilt feelings for not having been closer to them over the years. I'm not a perfect person.

I'm delighted to say that whenever I think of son, Chris, and his loving wife, Elizabeth, I just beam. Right now Marlita and I are on the highway to Chicago to spend a few days with them which is always a heartwarming experience. Elizabeth comes from a wonderful family where she was imbued with a spirit of helping others and living her faith. She's a preschool teacher in the Chicago public school system and is devoted to her students. I admire her selflessness.

Throughout my life I've known a lot of accomplished people but none more successful than Chris. Personality-wise he's very much like his mother, and I'm sure his late father would be enormously proud of the man that his son is. I know I am.

Chris graduated from Purdue and went on to earn his MBA at Duke. He's built a solid career and is the chief financial officer for a burgeoning financial tech company. My sense is that the two of them will never have to worry about money, and Marlita and I aim to always have their backs, especially now that Elizabeth's pregnant with their first child whom I've affectionately nicknamed "The Little Wombat." Don't ask me why. I tell them it's because wombats are adorable, and they haven't shared any potential baby names with us yet. I think Chris finds the nickname nutty but amusing, and Elizabeth is probably just too polite to call me an idiot to my face. I told you I have a rather quirky sense of humor, but that should be obvious by now.

But, I have another plan for the two of them and look forward to sharing the details this weekend. We cruise past Merrillville, Indiana, and Marlita calls Chris to say we'll be at their home in another forty-five minutes or so depending on traffic which is always a crap shoot in Chicagoland. Almost an hour later we finally arrive at their street in Lakeview, and Chris comes rushing out to assist with our bags.

"Here, Mom, let me help you with that! Hope you guys had an easy drive."

"Yeah, it was fine. We stopped in West Lafayette at Matt O'Neil's restaurant for lunch which is always delicious and saw your old college fraternity house. I bet that seems like eons ago now."

"Sure does. Ancient history. I hope you saved some room for dinner because we've made a dinner reservation at a very popular new restaurant on the lake. Between our busy work schedules and Liz's pregnancy, we've been staying home a lot more, so we're excited to try this new place out with you."

"Whatever you want to do is fine with us."

Elizabeth greets us at the door looking like a rose in bloom. "I'm so glad you came up," she says. "Once the baby's here, it'll probably be a little chaotic for a while."

"No 'probably' about it!" Marlita declares. "I told Nathan that we'll likely stay at an Airbnb close by after the baby comes."

"Aw, gee, and I was so hoping to learn how to change diapers!" I sarcastically announce.

"Not a problem, Pappy Nathan!" Chris assures. "You'll be a wiz in no time! I even have some YouTube videos you can watch!"

"Oh, swell!"

We hang out with them and their magnificent cat, Ollie, for a while just catching up, and then we call an Uber to take us to The Blue Wisp for dinner. It's a great meal but it hardly compares with the cuisine at the Monon Diner. I mean, what can you expect from entrees that ONLY cost sixty-freaking-dollars apiece! Jeez Louise!

After dinner we return to Liz and Chris's place and get comfy in the living room with Ollie. Chris pours us a couple of libations while Elizabeth abstains.

"There's something that your mom and I have given a lot of thought to that we'd like to share with you."

"Oh?!" Chris replies curiously.

I hesitate for a moment, then dive in. "Yeah, I've come into a bit of money recently, and I have an idea that I think is nothing short of brilliant!" I say modestly. "You know that most of my professional career was devoted to philanthropy for institutions in Cincinnati. I came to really admire the different ways that many people gave charitably. And, the more I learned about the role of community foundations, the more I thought about how you might enjoy the spirit of giving, especially through a donor-advised fund."

"Yeah, Nathan, that all sounds great, but you do know that we have a baby on the way, and we're also thinking of buying a house. I'm nervous enough about those huge obligations. As much as Liz and I would love to support more worthy causes, I just don't see it in the cards in the foreseeable future."

"Of course not. We totally understand that, so I took the liberty of speaking with the executive director of the Greater Chicago Community Foundation."

"I'm confused."

"Like I said I've come into a bit of money recently, well, actually it's a lot more than a bit, and your mom and I would like to establish The Christopher and Elizabeth Zyer Helton Donor Advised Fund from which you can recommend charitable gifts to organizations that you wish to support without having to go to the effort of maintaining your own charitable foundation."

"Gee! That really sounds lovely," Elizabeth effuses. "Thank you so much!"

"How much money are you guys thinking of funding it with?"

"We thought that an initial gift to the Chicago Community Foundation in the amount of $4 million might be a good start."

Chris nearly chokes on his bourbon. "Where in God's name did you ever come up with that kind of money?"

"Well, I could lie and say that I've saved my pennies and my book sales have really taken off, but the honest truth is they haven't."

"Did you rob a freaking bank?"

"Uh, no, but I did write something like that in one of my Clay Arnold novels."

"Seriously! Are you serious?! I mean, $4 million is a crazy amount. It would be nice to have money like that for a college fund for the 'little wombat' and for a nice house."

"We agree," Marlita adds. "That's why we're giving you another $4 million to help secure your family's future. The only thing we ask is that you please respect our wishes to keep this confidential for now. It's fine for you to tell your parents and brothers, Liz, but it's in everyone's best interest to not go shouting this from the rooftops, okay?"

"Wow!" Chris blurts out. "I mean, of course we'll respect your wanting us to stay mum about this, but we're stunned. Thank you!!!"

Marlita and I smile like a couple of Cheshire cats as we get copious hugs from the kids. I look at Elizabeth and worry that this announcement might send her into premature labor. Heaven forbid I'd have to learn how to change diapers sooner rather than later!

"Your mom and I love you both very much, and we want to be helpful, plus give you an opportunity to experience philanthropy. And, you don't need to give it away all at once. This'll give you an opportunity to do some research into which organizations you'd like to support and for how much."

"Man, I don't know what to say. I'm still flummoxed by where you ever came up with that kind of dough, Nathan."

"Well, life's a bit of a mystery sometimes, Christopher. We'll fill you in down the road, but for now, let's just enjoy the moment."

We spend the next thirty minutes basking in the glow of a happy family, and then we decide to call it a night. Ollie the Wonder Cat leads the way to our bedroom and then scoots off chasing some invisible prey. I turn to see Marlita beaming at me.

"So, how do you think the kids took our little announcement?!"

She wraps her arms around me, kisses my prominent proboscis, and playfully replies with one word…"flummoxed!"

"Oh! 'flummoxed' huh?! At least you didn't say gobsmacked!"

Chapter Nine

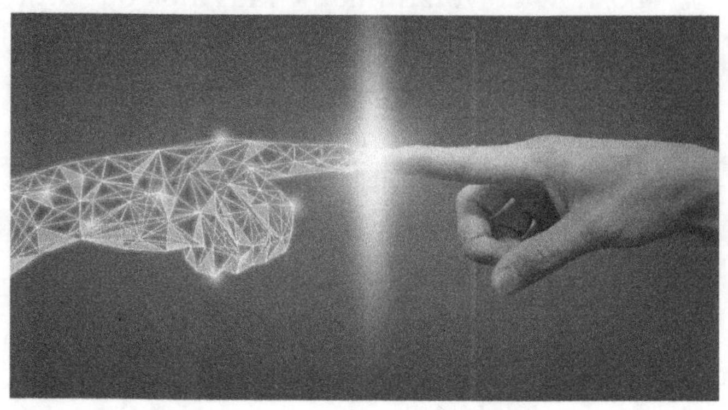

As a writer it's always fascinating to me where my inspiration comes from. Recollections of people that I knew twenty years ago and haven't spoken to since can come flooding back to me. Now that Marlita and I have put plans in place to financially help our family, I sit at my desk with Bella pondering who else we can share our good fortune with. I think of the title of my new book, *Given Names*, and reflect on a few people who've impressed me by how well they demonstrated the best virtues of humankind. My former colleague and dear friend, Suzanne, was the first person that came to mind.

~ Suzanne ~

It's dark and cold outside, and Suzanne Stanton has just finished a double shift in the open heart intensive care unit at the Jewish Hospital in Cincinnati, Ohio. To say that her work as a cardiovascular surgical nurse is lifesaving is accurate beyond words. Her last patient in the operating room was mere moments away from expiring on the table when Dr. Creighton and she miraculously pulled the fortunate soul back from the brink of death.

Now, sitting quietly in her car in the hospital's parking lot, she closes her eyes and thanks the Lord for giving her the medical skills and emotional fortitude to help heal the sick, something Suzanne has done now for over twenty years. It's been her mission in life and central to living her Christian faith. But, Suzanne's devotion to helping people in need doesn't end with her nursing career.

She slowly pulls her car out of the lot and drives through the neighborhood of Avondale toward East Walnut Hills. It's a route that she's driven scores of times over the years, through communities that are home to people of varying racial and economic backgrounds. As she sits at a traffic light looking at the looming gothic-style St. Francis de Sales church, she sighs and can't help but wonder if there's another chapter in her life that needs to be embraced. She's notices a teenage girl sitting alone in a darkened doorway leaning uncomfortably against a brick wall. The girl isn't dressed warmly enough for the dropping temperatures, and Suzanne pulls her car over to the curb to better see what her condition is. The girl is noticeably pregnant and staring vacantly into space as if lost to the world around her. Suzanne exits her car and slowly approaches the teenager who finally struggles to compose herself when she sees a stranger approaching.

"What do you want? Get away from me!"

"Hi, I'm a nurse, and I was driving home when I saw you sitting here alone in the cold."

"So! I don't need nuthin' from you." She rises and prepares to leave.

"Well, you may not, but your baby might. If you'll let me, I'll be happy to try to help you both."

The girl starts to cry and immediately wipes a tear away. "Get away from me!" she hurls again. "I don't need nobody's help."

"Is the baby's father helping you during your pregnancy?"

"Yeah right, fat chance of that! The last time I saw that loser he hit me and swore he was father to no damn baby. That was four months ago. Haven't seen him since."

"What about prenatal care? When was the last time you saw an obstetrician?"

"Now, how am I gonna pay for that?"

"There are clinics you can go to. I can help you find one in your neighborhood."

"Why you wanna do sumthin' like that? You don't know me. You don't owe me nuthin', and I sure as hell don't wanna owe you anything either!" She turns to leave again.

"How 'bout you come with me, and I can take you to where I live, get you something to eat, and a safe, warm place to sleep tonight? Then, tomorrow morning my friends and I can see about getting your baby and you some proper medical attention?"

For the first time the teenager looks Suzanne in the eye and begins to weep again. "Who're these friends you got? I can't be owing anybody anything, and why would y'all wanna help me anyway?"

"I live at a place called Harmony House, and in addition to being a nurse, I'm a nonvowed member of the Sisters of Mercy."

"What? You a Catholic nun or sumthin'?"

"Sorta, but I can still drink and have sex if I want because I haven't taken any vows of abstinence and chastity." They both smile at that.

"I don't know. I don't want anybody yammering at me about God and Jesus and stuff. I heard it all from my aunt, and it got old real fast. God don't care nuthin' about me probably because I dropped out of school and ain't got no job. It's just me and my baby, and we're livin' on the street."

"Well, if I promise you that no one will 'yammer' at you, would you be willing to come with me until we can get you and your baby checked out? Oh, and by the way, my name's Suzanne. You gotta name?"

"Course I got a name, although some people call me bitch or ho. Real name's Ruby though."

"Like the gem! I like that. Well, Ruby it's a pleasure to meet you. Now let's go get you somewhere safe and put some food in that budding belly of yours. I think you'll really like the women I live with."

Ruby's a little hesitant at first, but finally relents, and the two of them climb into Suzanne's car.

In the week that follows Ruby grows comfortable with her new friends, and Suzanne takes her to the Women and Infants Clinic where she receives a full physical exam and proper prenatal supplements.

It's not a one-sided experience though. Suzanne beams when she sees how well Ruby has adapted to the loving care she's receiving. She confides to her very close friend, Mary, "I love my career as a cardiovascular nurse, but I'm beginning to feel a real yearning to help more vulnerable young people like Ruby. Do you think the Mercy sisters and the diocese would help me start a program in

East Walnut Hills and Avondale where we can train these women to be nurses' aides to work in their own neighborhoods? It could be a real win/win!"

"I think it sounds like a splendid idea, Suzanne, and together, I think we should be able to convince them to fund a pilot program. After all, it's the kind of work we both believe God put us on this planet to do."

And that's what they did. Before long the Healing Covenant, under Suzanne's leadership, had blossomed into a thriving human services program helping many girls like Ruby fulfill lives that they never dreamed possible.

Word of Suzanne's successful community outreach model soon reached me in Indiana. Recalling Suzanne's loving spirit from our interactions during my fundraising career at the hospital, I wasn't the least bit surprised that she'd switched gears professionally and went on to again do very meaningful work. From time to time I saw posts on Facebook or read accounts on the internet of her program's success and the accolades that she received from many civic and religious leaders. She was living her faith, and I couldn't have been happier for her.

I made a decision and called Joe Daniels to ask his help. "Hey Joe, you remember Suzanne Stanton, don't you?"

Joe thinks for a moment. "Oh yeah, Suzanne Stanton, I remember her. She was an open heart surgery nurse when I was on the board of the hospital. Didn't she start that neighborhood program to train young women to be nurse aides?"

"She did, and I'd like to help her, Joe. Would you be willing to personally deliver a check from the charitable trust?"

"Of course, how much did you have in mind?"

"Well, I read that they needed more room than the St. Francis de Sales church could provide so Suzanne and her small board of directors are launching a capital campaign to buy a building and outfit it for training purposes and short-term living space."

"Any idea what the financial goal is for their campaign?"

"Not really, but I think $2 million might go a long way in funding their building needs and maybe providing a little endowment too. She really deserves our support, Joe. You got time to prepare a check and personally deliver it to Suzanne?"

"Sure thing. Do you want this to be anonymous, or can I tell her it's from you?"

I think for a moment. "Just tell her it's from an old friend from our Jewish Hospital days together who's always believed in her and coached her on how to raise dough. She'll know."

"Consider it done, Nathan."

A few days later Joe shows up unannounced at the offices of the Healing Covenant.

"Hello, I'm Joe Daniels. I'm an attorney with Hoffman Fabian and True. I was hoping to see Ms. Stanton. Is she available?"

"Is she expecting you, Mr. Daniels? She's awfully busy these days teaching classes to our young women."

"No, I don't have an appointment, but I promise not to take up too much of her time."

"Please give me a moment, sir, and I'll see if she has a few minutes to speak with you."

Three minutes later Suzanne steps out of her class and invites Joe to join her in her modest office. "Have we met before, Mr. Daniels? My assistant said you're an attorney. I sincerely hope we haven't done anything wrong that warrants legal action."

"On the contrary, Suzanne, I'm here at the request of a mutual friend and benefactor."

"Oh, I'm not sure who you mean."

"It's come to our attention that you're preparing to embark on a fundraising campaign to expand your organization's training facilities."

Suzanne has a bit of a perplexed expression on her face.

Joe continues and hands her an envelope which she opens. "We thought this gift might help you on your way."

Suzanne's eyes widen in astonishment when she sees a check made out to the Healing Covenant in the amount of $2 million.

"Oh my heavens! Is this real?"

Joe smiles and nods his head affirmatively. "It is, indeed!"

"I don't know what to say except thank you very much. Who's this from?"

Joe repeats essentially what Nathan had suggested to him. "Your benefactor asked me to simply say that's it's from an old friend from your hospital days who believes in you and used to counsel you on fundraising. Other than that he prefers to remain anonymous."

Suzanne thinks for a moment and a flash of recognition suddenly appears on her flushed face. She points to a black-and-white photograph of a birch tree on the wall behind her desk that she purchased from Nathan many years ago. His signature is in the lower right corner.

"Please tell him that he is and will forever be in my thoughts and prayers."

Chapter Ten

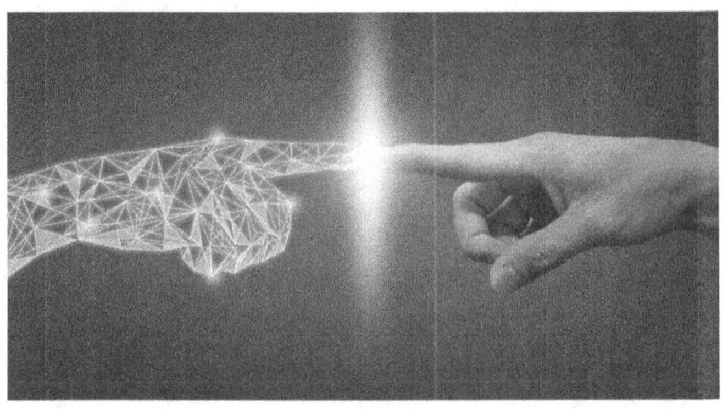

"NATHAN! NATHAN, ARE YOU UP THERE?" Marlita calls up to me from our living room.

"Yes, darling, I'm in my office writing. Do you need me to help you with something?"

A few moments later I see her smiling face appear in my office doorway. "There you are. What're writing?"

"Oh, I just wrote a new chapter to *Given Names*. Do you remember Suzanne Stanton? She was an open heart surgery nurse at the hospital. You met her when we were doing an art show at Summer Fair in Cincinnati."

"Yes, I remember Suzanne. She's the 'nunette' you're friends with. She stopped by our booth with her good friend, Sister Mary, right?"

"You've got a good memory, sweetie. Anyway, she's the first of the 'given names' I'm beginning to write about. I asked Joe Daniels to drop off a nice check to help her with their Healing Covenant capital campaign."

"Cool! I bet she really appreciated that. How much did you give her?"

"Two million."

"Wow, isn't it crazy we can talk about a big figure like that without blinking an eye?"

"Yeah, crazy's a good word for it, but she'll make great use of it."

"Speaking of identifying folks to support, have you talked with Stella recently to see if she has some ideas?"

"Just briefly, but I thought I'd have a late lunch at the Monon today after most everyone has cleared out and see if she has some suggestions. Do you want to come with me?"

"I'd love to, but I'm picking up the grandkids in Plainfield, and we're going to take a hike at McCormick's Creek. Enjoy your lunch, though, and let me know who Stella has in mind, okay?"

"Sure will. Give the kids a huge hug from Pappy Nathan!"

After Marlita leaves my office, I try to resume my writing but find that I'm distracted by other thoughts and choose not to force my next chapter. I've always believed that things will just flow when the time is right. So, I decide to putter around in the yard, doing my daily chores like making sure our chickens have plenty of food and fresh water and tackling my great, ever-present nemesis: weeding the garden beds around the house. On the one hand, I really don't enjoy weeding. Who does, right? But, on the other hand I find that some of my best literary thinking occurs when I'm mindlessly attacking dandelions and other verdant vagrants. Ya gotta love alliteration!

Marlita honks and waves to me as she pulls her Subaru out of the driveway. After slaving away for a while, I look at my watch and see that it's nearly one o'clock, so I figure I've done enough weeding for one day and return inside to get cleaned up. Thirty minutes later Pappy and I drive into town past the old J.J. Hunter caboose and park near the entrance to my favorite diner. There's just one other vehicle parked in front which means that Stella and I should probably have ample privacy to talk.

"Howdy, Nathan, it's great to see your smilin' face! Is it breakfast or lunch you're hankering for today?"

"I'm thinking your veggie frittata and coffee would hit the spot, and if you've got a few minutes I'd like to chat. And, by the way, it looks like you've made a few decorative changes here recently. You got a sugar daddy or sumthin?" We both smile at the private joke.

"Maybe," she lobs back at me coyly. "Give me a sec to take Lu and Herman's money, and we can sit a spell." Five minutes later she helps the elderly couple out the door and flips the sign to read closed.

"Life good?" I ask her as she brings my meal and sits down opposite me.

"No complaints here! I've been thinking about you and was hoping you'd drop by soon. I've got someone on my mind that I'd like to share with you."

"Oh? Anyone I know?"

"I'm not sure. Her name is Tess Monaco, and she comes in here for lunch from time to time. I think she rents a place over by Heritage Lake but comes to Greencastle often to help her customers."

"What kind of work does she do?"

"She works with a lot of older folks around town doing a little bit of everything from gardening to housekeeping, going to the grocery store, or taking them to medical appointments. She even looks after their pets. I think Tess basically got fed up working for other people and figured out how to make a good living working on her own terms."

"Is she married?'

"From what I gather she was married once, but it didn't work out. I think she's still single which surprises me because she's really a very pretty lady. I recall her telling me that she's definitely not gay but doesn't want any man telling her what to do. I think she just finds it easier to work hard and keep to herself."

"What else about Tess?"

"She's also a gourmet cook and a master gardener. She shared with me a while ago that her dream is to own a sweet little home with a lot of acreage so she could grow an enormous sunflower field and sell them all over the country."

"That's cool! So, what is it about her that you admire the most, and are you thinking that she's someone who deserves a good financial boost?"

"I do. She can outwork any three people, plus she's very devoted to her aged father and siblings, and she always has a bright smile on her face. I think Tess Monaco's a very special woman, and yeah, considering everything she does for everyone else, I think she's earned a bit of good fortune!"

~ Tess ~

Tess feels the warm sun on her face as she works the earth in the flower beds of the Evergreen Nursing Home. The combination of the loamy soil and invigorating sunlight provides an enriching feeling for her both physically and emotionally. Family members come and go visiting their loved ones, and the presence of her vivid flowers seems to help brighten the experience for everyone. She takes great pride in keeping the beds virtually weed-free accentuating the hues of the blossoms and shrubs.

"Lookin' good there, little lady!" her supervisor chirps at her, "And, the flowers are very pretty too."

Tess nods her head at Maurice. "Thank you," she replies evenly. "I think I'll have these beds finished before too long."

"Yep, you look good in that bed," he praises. "Yep, mighty good! I bet you look right fine in other beds too."

Tess ignores his chauvinistic remark and stays focused on the job at hand. It's not the first time Maurice has made some sort of inappropriate remark which she usually dismisses but is getting increasingly weary of hearing. She needs the work but not the disrespect.

"Let me know when you're finished out here so I can inspect, uh, your work. I've got something else I'd like you to do too."

Tess nods her head in acknowledgment as she plants a freshly prepared plot with New Guinea Impatiens. Ten minutes later Maurice comes out again and leers at her from behind.

"Ain't you finished yet?"

Tess is startled by his unexpected presence and obnoxious question. "I didn't know you were standing there."

"Yeah, well, I like to privately watch my workers to make sure they're doing stuff the way I like it."

"Okay, I think I'm nearly done with these flowers," she replies as she brushes the soil off her jeans. "I'll just pack my yard tools and this bag of manure in my truck and be on my way soon."

"Well, hold on there, little lady. There's something else I want you to do for me."

"What's that, Maurice?"

"I need some work done at my place too. I was thinking you could stop by later this evening and give me a hand. Might even be a few beers in it for ya if you're good."

"I don't think that's a very good idea. I work for Evergreen and not for you, besides I'm tired and dirty."

"Oh, I like women that are a little tired and dirty." He walks over to Tess and puts his hand on her waist.

"Hey, get your hand off me, and don't ever do that again."

"Now, what kind of piss-poor attitude is that. All I want is a little, uh, special attention, Tessie."

Tess stares at her sexist boss and looks around to see if anyone is around. "Okay, Maurice, but just this one time but never again. Undo your trousers and close your eyes."

Good ol' Maurice can't believe he's gonna actually get the special attention that he feels he's entitled to and does as she instructs.

"Ready when you are, Tessie!"

The next thing he feels and smells is the aroma of fresh, stinky, nasty manure as Tess dumps an entire bag on that prick, Maurice.

"Aaarrrggghhh! Why'd you have to go and do that?"

"How's that feel, Jerk-weed?! 'Cause that's the only special attention you'll ever get from me, and by the way, I quit!"

As Tess climbs into her truck, she hears a visitor who's just stepped outside say to her young daughter, "Avert your eyes, Clarabelle, this apparently isn't the sort of place for grandma after all!"

Two days later Tess pulls into the parking lot of the Monon Diner for a late dinner. She's just finished a long day helping Mrs. Kissinger and doesn't have the energy to pick up groceries at Barney's and prepare a meal.

"Welcome, Tess!" Stella says warmly. "You're not cooking one of your gourmet dinners tonight I take it."

"No, not tonight, Stella, I'm just too pooped to putter around in the kitchen, so I thought I'd treat myself to your good cooking."

"It's always great to see you. Listen, I was wondering if you'd have some time to take a little drive with me when you're finished here. It's still gonna be light out for a while, and there's something I'd really like to show you."

"I don't know about tonight, Stella. I love Mrs. K. beyond words, but she darn near wore me out."

"Well, what I want to show you is pretty near your place, and we can drive separately so you can head on home from there."

After a wholesome dinner and a piece of peach pie, Tess says, "Okay, Stella, I guess I can spare a few minutes especially if it's near my place. You lead the way."

The drive takes twenty minutes, and Tess wonders where the heck Stella is taking her. They approach Heritage Lake, turn off the county road into a secluded driveway, and come upon a charming cottage-like home adjacent to a twenty-acre field that Tess has never seen before. It's a yellow wooden frame house with white trim and flower boxes adorning the windows. There's a sold real estate sign in the home's front yard, and Stella and Tess park their vehicles in the gravel driveway.

"C'mon, let's go inside and take a look."

"We can't go in there, Stella, the sign reads that it's been sold."

"It's all right, Tess, I know the new owner."

Tess is understandably very confused but joins Stella as they enter the lovely home. Tess's eyes grow wide with wonder as she sees how nicely the interior of the home is appointed, and she gasps with delight when she sees that the kitchen has all of the appliances and accoutrement befitting a gourmet cook.

"Wow! This place is amazing, but I'm confused Stella. Are you in the real estate business now too?"

"No, believe me, I have my hands full running the Monon." They wander around the interior, and Tess sees that the two full bathrooms have contemporary designs and fixtures. Then, they enter the primary bedroom, and Stella leads her over to a large picture window which reveals a wonderful panoramic view of twenty acres of freshly tilled fields.

"Pretty special place!" Tess says wistfully. "A lot nicer than my little apartment." She turns to face Stella who has her hand outstretched holding an envelope.

"What's this?" Tess asks befuddled.

"Open it!" Stella replies with a warm smile on her face.

Tess hesitates a sec and then opens the envelope. It's a deed to the house and property with Tess Monaco listed as the owner.

Tess sighs and says sadly, "I'm sorry, Stella, but I can't afford this."

"It's yours free and clear, compliments of a friend who wishes to remain anonymous and only asks that you keep this gift confidential."

"But, I don't understand! I don't have to sleep with him, do I?"

"No, of course not! He's a gentleman. But wait, there's more." Stella pulls out a second envelope and hands it to her revealing a cashier's check in the amount of $500,000 made out in Tess's name.

Tess nearly falls to the floor in shock. "Stella, is this all real? I mean, how is this possible?"

"Yes, it's very real, and it all belongs to you. Your benefactor wishes to remain silent and asked me to be the conduit in thanking you for all of the hard work and goodness you bring to so many people every single day!"

Tess begins to weep with perplexed joy. "I don't know what to say. I'm just so overwhelmed."

"Good! 'Overwhelmed' is good! But, there's one more thing I want to show you. C'mon!"

Stella leads Tess outside, and they walk toward the entrance of the large field. The sun is getting lower in the western sky casting a golden glow on the fallow field. They stand next to a large wooden sign with a muslin cover over it. Stella slowly unties the cords holding the cover in place revealing words that Tess never dreamed possible:

Tess Monaco's Sunflower Farm
Bringing Bountiful Blossoms to the World

Chapter Eleven

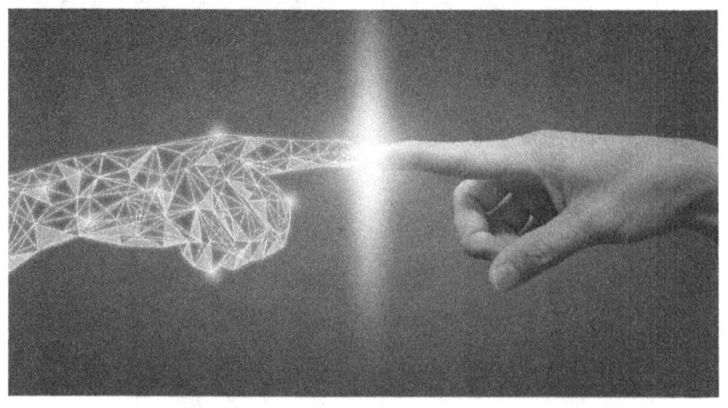

I AWAKE EARLY IN THE MORNING thinking about the next chapter for my book, *Given Names*. The intriguing challenge I've always contended with as a writer is composing what comes next in the story. With my newly found wealth, it would be easy for me to chuck it all and spend my time just buying stuff or thinking of creative ways to give money away. Fact of the matter is I just love writing, and when my thoughts flow, I feel true contentment. I keep a handwritten sheet of paper on my desk with the names of people and places that Marlita and I may choose to support, and I try to decide which one would be an exciting subject for the next chapter in my novel…and in my life. Thankfully, there's a lot to choose from which makes me think that I'm probably less of a snarky cynic than I tell people I am.

It's only about seven o'clock, but I pick up my phone and call Joe Daniels in Cincinnati. The phone rings twice, and I hear my consiglieri's voice.

"It's gotta be you, Nathan. No one else calls me this early unless it's a client with some sad family news."

"Good morning, Joseph, I knew you'd be up. Just wanted to touch base with you."

"Right, I take it this means that Marlita's still asleep and you wanted someone to talk with."

"Bingo! Even Bella's got more entertaining things to do this morning than listen to my blarney. So, I've been thinking about some things I want to share with you if you've got a sec."

"Share away, mon ami!"

I begin by telling him about the gifts to Tess Monaco. "Stella phoned me last evening as she was leaving Tess and heading back to Greencastle. She was so excited and kept going on and on about how overwhelmed Tess was by her new home and the prospect of starting her new sunflower business. We did a good thing, Joe!"

"That's wonderful, Nathan, and how is the lovely Stella?"

"I think she's a pretty happy lady these days. She asked me if I'd heard from you and was wondering when you might be returning to Greencastle."

"Hmmm…Interesting," Joe muses.

"Yeah, I thought so too. Back in my pre-Marlita days if I'd known how far kissing a girl's hand and spouting a little French would get me, I'd be wearing a beret and crooning like Leonard Cohen."

We change subjects and get down to some serious business. "So, what's on your mind, Nathan?"

"Marlita and I have been doing a lot of cogitating about organizations in our Putnam County community, and I was thinking of asking you to prepare a couple of checks and come here to deliver some surprise gifts."

"Sounds great to me. Which organizations are you thinking of and when did you have in mind?"

"Well, Marlita and I were talking about how many times people have dumped their unwanted cats and dogs on our property over the years, believing we'd take care of them, and sure enough, they were right. I shudder to think how much time we spent trying to find new owners, or the money we've spent on vet bills for strays, but it's always been the right thing to do. Now, with the resources we have, we're thinking of making a statement about how we want our community to care for our unwanted four-legged friends."

"Sounds very humane, Nathan! What other organization did you have in mind?"

"So, the more we talked about 'thrown-away' animals, the more we began to think about people who are down on their luck and have no place to stay. It's so heartbreaking to even think about it, so yeah, we'd like to be helpful with our homeless shelter too."

"Any idea about how much you guys want to contribute to each?"

"You know, Joe, given how much we have and how much more we'll have from investment income, it's crazy not to be generous. Marlita and I were thinking about a million dollars each, at least to begin with."

"Okay, let me make certain I have the exact legal names for both shelters and the names of their directors. I'll prepare a couple of checks, and once you and I look at our calendars, I'll make a couple of calls to schedule some appointments. When's a good time for you, Nathan?"

"Well, you're the working stiff, Joe. You tell me when you're available. You're always welcome to bunk with us for as long as you want." I hear him hum as he looks at his calendar.

"I've got an important board meeting coming up for the Underground Railroad Freedom Center on Thursday that I need to prepare for. How about the next day?"

"Works for us, Joe, we'll see you on Friday then." We chat a moment longer and then hang up.

~ The Homeless Shelter ~

Cade Willet knows he has an addictive personality. In his younger years he regularly smoked twenty cigarettes a day and tried to quit a couple of times only to get sucked back into the nasty habit. Now, he's up to nearly two packs a day with no big desire to give it up. And, as if cigarettes aren't bad enough, alcohol now has a tight grip on him that he just can't, or won't, shake. Cade deludes himself into believing he can kick his habits any time if he just sets his mind to it, but he enjoys the stupid satisfaction of nicotine and the numbing escape that booze gives him. He's hooked, and his addiction has caused a ton of heartache for his family.

Cade loves his three children and used to love his wife until she gave him an ultimatum to quit drinking or she was gonna leave him. And, that's exactly what 'that dang bitch' did. She divorced him and has full custody of their kids. He also lost his house in the process that his ex-wife now shares with some other dude. And sadly, he's about to lose his job too.

In the parking lot outside of his job at the zinc mill, Cade pours down half a bottle of vodka and staggers out of his truck to start his 7:00 a.m. shift. He goes into the men's room to take a leak and pulls his fingers through his matted hair like a comb. He notices that his shirt isn't buttoned correctly, and he grunts, "screw it" after failing to fix it twice. He heads over to the heavy machinery area where he drives a forklift most days, but his immediate supervisor stops him before he climbs inside the lift. "Good to see you made it on time today, Cade. Looks like you had a wild night last night."

"Yeah, just staying up late playing pickleball with some buddies," he lies.

"Had yourself a few tugs on the bottle, too, I imagine?"

"Yeah, well, it ain't pickleball unless you get a little 'pickled' afterward," he laughs. He stumbles as he begins to climb into the forklift, and his supervisor, Lonnie, says, "Hey, easy goes it, buckaroo, are you sure you're in decent enough shape to work today? Remember the boss was pretty pissed off the other day when you ran into the side of our dump truck."

"I'll be all right."

Just then Lonnie's phone beeps. It's the big boss, Mr. Cliburn. *Tell Mr. Willet I need to see him in my office...pronto!*

Lonnie relays the message to Cade who slides off the forklift seat and walks toward the shop office.

"Close the door and don't bother sitting down, Cade, this won't take long."

"What's up, boss?"

"I watched you trip as you were getting into the forklift, Cade. Are you drunk again? You remember what I told you about drinking on the job, don't ya?"

"Yessir, I just had me a little nip out in the lot before I came in," Cade says sheepishly as he tries to focus on Mr. Cliburn's face through bleary eyes.

"I'm sorry, Cade, but I gotta let you go. You're too much of a risk to be working here drunk."

"You're firing me, Mr. Cliburn? I can't afford to lose this job. I don't got no where to go or even to sleep at night."

"I'm sorry," Cade," he repeats, "but I'm not running a social agency here, and my insurance company will cancel my policy if I file any more claims for damages. You need to collect your stuff and go. Maybe the homeless shelter will take you in until you can get yourself straightened out. That's it. Close the door on your way out."

Cade accepts his dismissal and walks out the door without closing it. He shuffles across the shop floor and ambles out into the parking lot where he struggles to remember where he parked his truck. He finally finds it and climbs inside. "What now?" he wonders aloud. He recalls Mr. Cliburn's suggestion about the homeless shelter and figures it's probably a free, safe place to crash for a few hours. He knows where it's located and somehow manages to drive there without causing harm to people or property.

Cade walks inside the shelter and sees that there are a ton of people lying around everywhere, mostly women with young children, but a couple of much older people too. He spies a closed door that bears a small sign that reads *office*. Without knocking he pushes the door open and sees a meeting in progress. The meeting is between Joseph Daniels and the homeless shelter's director, Rebecca Lind.

"Excuse me, sir, but we're in the middle of a meeting. Would you kindly step outside until we're done? Thank you."

"Yes, ma'am, but I just lost my job and need a place to stay. You gotta room I can crash in for a little while. I promise not to be any trouble. I just need to catch me a couple of winks, ma'am."

Joe watches the exchange take place, and Ms. Lind gets up from her desk to help escort Cade out the door. "We just don't have any room, sir. I'm not trying to be unkind, but you can see that we have people sleeping in the halls and on the porches. We're just crowded beyond lawful capacity."

Cade nods his head in resignation and exits the office.

"I'm sorry for the interruption, Mr. Daniels, but as you can see we're just not in a position to help everyone that comes our way. Now, can you please tell me the reason for your visit? We're generally visited by people in dire need rather than nicely dressed attorneys."

"I understand, and I appreciate the dilemma that you and your shelter are facing. I'm here at the request of my client who wishes to remain anonymous. He is a person who is sympathetic to the challenges you face, and I believe we're in a position to be of some assistance." Joe hands Ms. Lind an envelope and watches as her eyes grow wide with stupefaction as she sees a check made payable to the homeless shelter in the amount of $1 million.

"I trust that you may find this gift useful, Ms. Lind. My client and I have only two conditions for receiving this gift."

Rebecca Lind nods her head affirmatively but is too stunned to utter words other than: "Of course."

"These conditions are: (1) That you share the details of this with no one other than your board of directors and that you advise them to maintain the utmost in confidentiality; and (2) that you please find that man who was just in your office and arrange suitable lodging for him, at a motel if necessary, until such time that you can find space for him here or elsewhere. Are we agreed, Ms. Lind?"

"Uh, yes! Of course. Thank you so much, Mr. Daniels, and please thank your client. This is like manna from heaven for us."

"I shall. My client also instructed me to say that it's very possible that your shelter could receive continuing support as well…now, please, go and find that man!"

Chapter Twelve

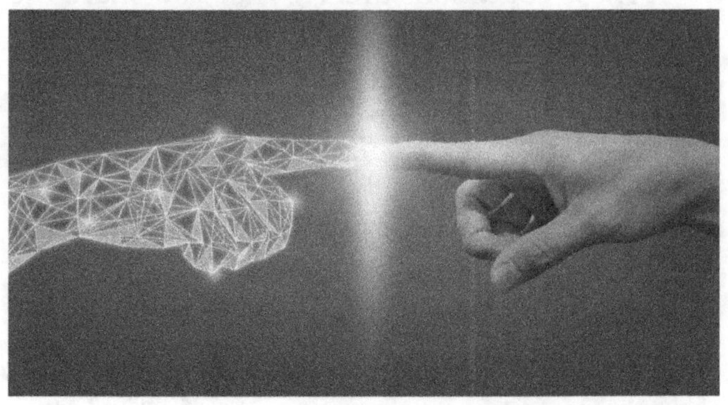

AFTER HIS MEETING at the homeless shelter, Joe drives back to our home and joins Marlita and me on the porch for a libation and some of my witty banter. To be perfectly frank, Marlita has never found my quick-witted repartee particularly amusing, and Joe, well, I think he's just being polite. It's clear I need to come up with some new audiences… or maybe some new material…or maybe just quit telling my father's old jokes.

"How'd it go at the homeless shelter, Joe?' Marlita asks.

"It went as you might expect when some stranger shows up and lays a cool million dollar check on you. Ms. Lind was understandably baffled, flummoxed, bewildered, perplexed, and maybe even a little gobsmacked too!"

"Oh, for Garfield's sake! Not you, too, Joe! Enough with the big, dumbass words!"

Joe and I look at each other with conspiratorial smiles. "Pardon me, Marlita, Nathan's sophisticated vocabulary is highly contagious!"

In the interest of domestic tranquility, I wisely change the subject to something far more plebeian. "Who's hungry?! Anyone up for a trip to the Monon?!"

"I'm game," Joe immediately replies. "How about you, Marlita? Care to join us this time?"

"I would, but I have to teach a yoga class in a few minutes. Besides, Joe, I wouldn't want to cramp your continental style with Stella Chastain."

We hang out on the porch for a few minutes longer, and then Joe and I sashay out to the carport and climb into Pappy. We pull out of the driveway just in the nick of time as a caravan of Marlita's yoga students is only seconds away from driving onto our property. I wave to each car as we head for dinner.

"You know we have other nice restaurants in Greencastle, don't you, Joe? Is it the cuisine or the queen of the cuisine that you've got a hankering for?"

Joe deftly dodges my question and artfully alters the subject to business.

"So, Nathan, I have the other check for the animal shelter back at your house. I've scheduled an appointment tomorrow morning with the director, a guy named Gus Miles. Do you know him?"

"Yeah, I know Gus. Not very well, but he recently retired as a biology professor at Asbury College. I think the county's really lucky to have someone with his background. Keeping the shelter financially viable had been a very frustrating challenge until the county and state finally agreed to pony up with enough dough to pay for proper facility maintenance and solid professional staffing. Despite that fiscal underpinning, though, they really need to expand the size of the shelter and upgrade their presence online to keep folks aware of the cats and dogs available for adoption."

"So, that's where you come in, right?"

"Yeah, this is something that's particularly important to Marlita, and we're both curious to learn what their plans are for the future. We want to be very helpful, especially now that someone with Gus Miles's credentials is at the helm."

I steer Pappy past the blue J.J. Hunter caboose and pull into the Monon's parking lot. I see only one vehicle that I immediately recognize. It's a late model gold Lexus sedan, and it belongs to my great pal, Joanne. I say "Joanne," but given her Pennsylvania Dutch heritage everyone, including me, calls her "Dutch."

As Joe and I begin to enter the door, an elderly couple that I ran into here a few weeks back starts to exit. They both try to go through the door at the same time, and it looks like an old vaudeville routine.

"Look, Rufus, it's that smart writer feller that we saw here before."

"Don't look that smart to me, Maude! Neither does the guy he's with. I bet they don't have a workin' brain between the two of 'em."

"You'll have to pardon my husband, gentlemen. He gets a little 'ornery' when his blood sugar spikes."

"I ain't 'horny,' Maude. Quit makin' up stories. I swear your hearing gets worser and worser with each passin' day."

Maude thanks Joe as he holds the door open for them. "Please excuse my husband."

"Now, why the heck did you tell them to 'execute' your husband?" Rufus asks petulantly. "I swear you're gettin' a little mental on me too!" Maude points to her temple as if to imply that good ol' Rufus ain't exactly right-in-the-head.

Joe and I wait patiently as the octogenarians shuffle through the doorway and into the parking lot. We watch as Maude has to guide Rufus away from getting in the wrong car.

"Now, you know where my literary inspiration comes from, Joe. It's all around me!"

"I'm sure Mark Twain would've had a field day here!"

We enter the Monon and see Stella talking to my pal Dutch and a table full of her lady chums. "C'mon, Joe, you've gotta meet these gals. They're a hoot!"

Stella starts to blush as we approach their table, and turns even redder when Joe gives her a little peck on both cheeks.

"We meet again, dear lady. Always a pleasure to be in your establishment and to see your pulchritude. How've you been?"

Dutch and her buddies stop eating and giggle as they witness the warm exchange between Stella and Joe.

"Welcome back, Joe," she coos. "Was wondering when you might return."

"Joe, I want you to meet Dutch Vanderhaar and her daughter, Lisette, and their partners in mischief-making, Judith, Barbara, Beth, and Sally. Ladies, this is my good friend, Joe Daniels, from Cincinnati."

They're all initially on their best behavior with polite words of welcome to Joe, and then Beth blurts out, "Well, hell's bells, Stella, I'll take 'im if you're not interested."

Now it's Dutch's turn to blush. "Uh, filters, Beth! You remember what we talked about earlier about using filters in public!"

I change the subject. "So, what's the occasion for your gathering today, ladies?"

Lisette replies, "It's actually a bittersweet occasion. It's mom's birthday today, but we had to put our little dog, Wags, down yesterday."

"Poor little guy just finally ran out of steam. He was such a great friend, and I miss him so much," Dutch laments with a tear in her eye.

"Well, congratulations on your birthday, but I'm very sorry about your pup. I remember Wags very well, and I'm really sorry he's gone, Dutch. You still have your cat, Mister Whiskers, don't you?"

"I do, but it's just not the same…Poor Wagsy!"

We chat just a moment longer, and then Stella leads Joe and me to a table. "So, how do you know these ladies, Nathan?"

"Oh, Dutch and I became good friends through our volunteer work together for the Greencastle Summer Music Festival. We both served on the board of directors and helped build up the festival's endowment fund at our community foundation. She and Lisette and their family actually started the endowment fund in memory of Dutch's husband, and then I kicked in a few bucks and used some of my old fundraising skills to lean on a few other folks. We've remained pals ever since, and Dutch has been a good buddy with these other gals forever."

Over the next hour we enjoy a leisurely dinner and the crowd eventually starts to thin out. I walk over to Dutch as she prepares to leave and whisper, "There's something I'd like to talk with you about in the next couple of weeks, so if you can find some time for us to chat…"

"Oh, dear boy, I might be able to fit you into my busy schedule," she laughs. "I'll check my calendar and get back to you, okay?" She gives me a sweet hug and rejoins her partners-in-mischief.

Stella finally gets a few secs and sits down with Joe and me. "You know, I'm not sure if you're aware of it, Stella, but you and Joe share an important role in my and Marlita's lives."

"Oh? Is that 'role' something that requires absolute secrecy and a modicum of integrity?"

"Indeed, it does," I reply. "Stella, you're my confidant and agent for giving gifts to some people, and Joe is my attorney, trustee, and agent for giving money to charitable organizations. The two of you are the public faces of our philanthropy."

"We're very honored, Nathan, aren't we, Stella?" he says as he lightly pats her hand.

"Honored…and grateful, Joe! So, are you here on business for Nathan and Marlita?"

Joe glances at me for affirmation and replies with a confirming nod. "I am. Have an appointment with Gus Miles scheduled for tomorrow morning at the animal shelter."

"Shame you're working, Stella," I interject. "Could be fun for the two of you to make that meeting together."

"Well, it just so happens that we're closed on Monday, Nathan, so I'd be happy to join you, Joe… if you're serious."

"Sounds great, Stella, why don't I meet you here at, say, around ten o'clock, and you can show me where it is."

"It's a date," she begins to say, but quickly tries to self-correct and says, "It's a day to remember."

~ Animal Shelter ~

The next morning Joe arrives promptly at the Monon and sees Stella outside watering baskets of hanging flowers near the entrance.

"Always working, aren't you?!"

"Got to. The place doesn't run itself. Just give me a sec, and I'll be ready to go."

A few minutes later Stella climbs into Joe's Audi and sinks into the rich Corinthian leather seats. "Ooh, nice ride, Joe, we don't see a lot of these around here."

"Yeah, I like it because it's comfortable for long drives, and my clients seem to enjoy it. In the end, it's really just a car, though, something to get me from point A to point B."

Stella directs Joe to drive south on Jackson Street and hang a left at the courthouse square. "I reckon Nathan's shown you a bunch of the town already, but sing out if there's some place you'd like to see."

"Nathan's shown me around some, but if you've got some special places to show me, I'll have a little bit of time after our meeting, then I'll need to drop you off and head back to Cincinnati. No doubt,

Nathan and Marlita will want me to come back soon, so if not today, perhaps the next time I come to town we can cruise around."

"Well, let me think about some choice places, Joe. The covered bridges are definitely cool, and I know some great country roads. For now, though, let's go make somebody's day at the animal shelter."

We cruise through the square, then past Barney's grocery store and the hardware store. "Just keep heading east, Joe, we'll be on the outskirts of town once we pass Walmart, and then the animal shelter is just a few miles beyond that. You'll see their sign and gate on the right."

Joe sees the open gate for the animal shelter, and the cacophonous sound of barking dogs erupts as he parks his Audi by the main building. He and Stella get out and are greeted by a young woman who's hosing down one of the enclosed runs.

"G'morning!" Joe shouts above the sound of the dogs and the hose. "We're here to see Gus Miles? Is he inside?"

"Don't know for sure. I got in here around seven this morning, but I haven't seen him yet. I've been pretty busy though. You might try his office."

Joe and Stella walk inside and see another young woman manning the front desk. Her name badge reads *Heidi*. "Good morning, I'm Joe Daniels and this is Stella Chastain, we have an appointment to see Mr. Miles this morning."

"He didn't contact you earlier?"

"No, why?" Stella asks.

"He called me late last night. His mother was rushed to the hospital with congestive heart failure, I think. Gus was pretty concerned about her. He asked me to check his calendar when I got in this morning, and to reschedule any appointments he had for today. I guess I forgot to do that. I'm really sorry."

"Oh, I'm very sorry to hear about his mother. I hope she'll be all right," Joe offers. "Ms. Chastain and I have something very important we wanted to deliver to him personally. Any idea if he'll be back later today?"

"Hard to tell. He said his mom is scheduled for surgery this morning, so my guess is he'll stay at the hospital for most of the day."

"I'm an attorney and have a very important document for Mr. Miles. Do you have a very secure place where you can put it, or are we better off coming back another time?"

"We have a safe," Heidi suggests. It's open now, and I could lock it in there. No one knows the combination but Gus. I think it should be very secure in there, and I'll be sure to let him know that you brought the document for him."

Stella and Joe look at each other to ascertain the other's opinion about leaving a million dollar check. "I could always cancel payment if necessary," Joe whispers to Stella. She nods her head in agreement, and they decide to hand the envelope over to Heidi.

"You'll be certain that Mr. Miles gets this, right?" Stella makes her point.

"Yes, ma'am, I won't forget this time. I promise I'll lock it up right after you leave."

Joe hands Heidi his business card. "Please ask Mr. Miles to give me a call when he comes in."

"Will do, sir. Just as soon as he comes in."

Stella and Joe thank her and begin to exit the office door when they're confronted by a uniformed officer.

"That your car out there?" Officer Snurd asks brusquely.

"Yes, officer, it is. Why? Is something wrong?"

"I noticed that your license plates are due to expire this month. You need to take care of that."

Both Stella and Joe look at each other with bemused disbelief at being challenged over the license plate on the Audi. Joe looks at the officer's badge and name tag and sees that Officer Snurd is actually the animal control officer apparently assigned to the shelter.

"Thank you, Officer Snurd, but I believe my license plate and registration are still current. I mailed my annual registration fee to the Ohio Department of Transportation last week and am awaiting the new one to arrive."

"Yeah, well, see to it that you do! If you return here and it's expired, I'll have to cite you." Heidi looks on nervously.

"Sir, I mean no disrespect, but why would an animal control officer be so concerned about my license plate?"

"Cuz I'm a county sheriff deputy, and we take such matters very seriously."

"That's impressive, Officer! We sure need more animal control personnel like you on the job! You never know when one of us human animals is going to seriously break the law!" Joe replies with a smile. "Right, Ms. Chastain?!"

"Yep! You betcha, Mr. Daniels!" They say good-bye to Heidi again, sidle past the petulant officer, and exit the building.

Officer Snurd watches the Audi drive away and turns to Heidi who was privately delighted in seeing the officer get politely eviscerated.

"What'd those people want?"

"Uh, they had an appointment with Mr. Miles. Gus couldn't keep the appointment because his mother's in the hospital."

Heidi starts to place the envelope that Joe gave her in the safe, but Officer Snurd sees the attorney's name on the envelope. "They give you that?" He roughly asks Heidi.

She doesn't answer him immediately, and he snatches the envelope from her hand.

"Hey, that's not for you. Give it back! I told them I'd lock it in the safe until Gus returns."

Officer Snurd rips open the envelope and sees a letter from Joseph Daniels, Esquire to Mr. Miles, and then he sees the check in the amount of $1 million payable to the Putnam County Animal Shelter. His eyes go wide in disbelief.

"Give it back!" she demands again, but Officer Snurd puts it in his pocket. "This here's official county business. I'll take care of it." And then he walks out the door.

Chapter Thirteen

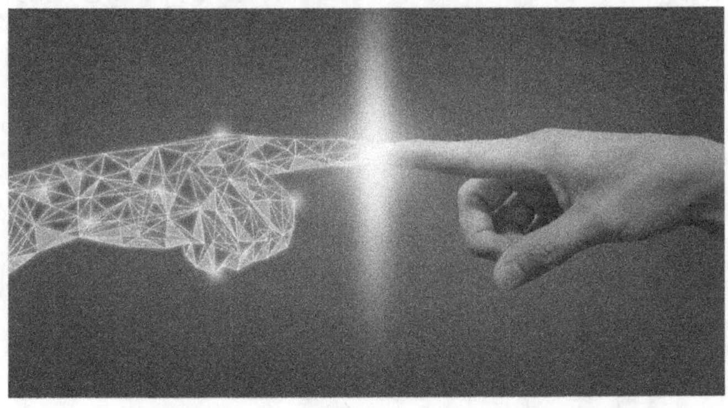

GET A CALL FROM JOE telling me that Gus Miles wasn't able to keep the appointment with Stella and him. "We ended up leaving the check and my cover letter with an employee in the office who said she'd lock it in the safe. Stella and I debated just leaving it with her, but I saw the safe and figured we could always cancel payment on the check if something nefarious were to occur."

"Sounds reasonable, but isn't it nice to see the look on someone's face when they get that kind of financial windfall?"

"Yes, it is, Nathan, something very exciting, indeed! I dropped Stella off a couple of minutes ago at the Monon, and now I'm heading back to Cincinnati. I have a meeting among my law partners tomorrow morning, and I imagine we'll all be subjected to the same old drone about billable hours and a possible consolidation with another major law firm."

"Sounds like a barrel of laughs, Joe. When are you going to dump that gig and live the life you want? Hell, you've got enough dough, and Marlita and I try to be reasonable clients."

"You are extremely reasonable clients, and yes, thanks to you and my own savings, I have enough money to go the distance, I think. I've been practicing law in a prestigious firm for so long that a lot of my personal identity is tied up in it. Besides, I've had generations of clients that still rely on me."

"I understand, and you wouldn't be the Joseph Daniels we all admire if you didn't struggle against dramatically changing your current lifestyle. You're part of the fabric of numerous charitable organizations in Cincinnati, and anyway, I'm just thinking out loud, Joe. I'll tell you this, though, I've never regretted ditching my former life, no matter how fulfilling it was at times, and taking up roots with Marlita where no one else knows my name."

"It's worked for you very well, hasn't it, Nathan? It's something to ponder."

While we're on the phone, I give Joe the names of a few other charities I'd like him to do some research on regarding their financial viability and strength of their management. Some are here in Putnam County, and some are in Cincinnati. "Good luck with your meeting with the partners tomorrow, Joe, I hope it goes well for you." We hang up.

~ Tammy ~

It's curious which memories of my former fundraising life in Cincinnati come back to me. I was very fortunate to represent fine institutions like Children's Hospital, The Jewish Hospital, and the Cincinnati Zoo and Botanical Gardens. I took my responsibilities very seriously. It was also very important to me to help train and guide my colleagues representing other institutions in fundraising techniques and ethics. So, I was honored when they elected me as president of two professional trade associations: The Ohio Association for Hospital Development and the Greater Cincinnati Planned Giving Council.

I'll never forget feeling chagrined and a little pissed off when a prominent philanthropist once told me that all a charitable organization needed in the way of fundraising staff was "a pretty blond girl in a convertible." To be honest, there were a few development officers and agency executives that I met over the years that were amiable, but in my opinion were darn lucky to have their jobs. In the main, however, most were dedicated professionals. Then, every once in a while there were very special people who came along who knew how to listen and actually followed the counsel that I offered. A few went on to be great leaders. Tammy Kaplan was such a person.

I didn't know Tammy in the beginning, but she knew my reputation and called me one day and asked to get together to talk about raising money and how to build a charitable organization from the ground up. She had a vision and a personal *raison d'être* that I was soon to learn about.

———

"Hi Nathan, I'm Tammy Kaplan. It's very nice to finally meet you! A mutual friend suggested that you'd be a good resource to chat with about an idea I have."

I returned her salutation and offered, "If I can help, I'll be happy to. Who's our mutual friend?"

"Miriam Timmer."

"Ah yes, a great lady and a very good friend. We worked together on a major fundraising gala for the hospital a while back. She had a great knack for keeping the volunteers in the hospital auxiliary focused on the project. No easy task, I can assure you! I haven't seen Mimi in a while which is something I must correct."

We sat down for lunch at a trendy restaurant in Hyde Park and eyed each other as we got seated, trying to form accurate first impressions. My immediate impression was that Tammy was a kind soul who also exuded a certain wisdom. I was immediately curious about the direction our conversation would go.

"How can I help, Tammy?"

"I need your help, Nathan, in suggesting ways to build a new organization in Greater Cincinnati that'll provide a place for cancer patients and their loved ones to gather and learn and share their experiences. There's a national organization called the The Healing Community that's doing amazing work, and I want to begin an organization locally."

I don't know about you, but when I hear the word *cancer, i*t scares the bejesus out of me, which caused me to take Tammy very seriously.

"So, where do you stand in the process so far?"

"Well, I've written our Articles of Incorporation for the state of Ohio, and our application to become a tax-exempt 501(c)(3) charitable organization has just been granted…and I've drafted our mission statement and bylaws."

"Wow, you already done a lot! I'm very impressed. How about people to serve on your board and prospects to provide major financial support?"

"Yeah, I've managed to recruit a cadre of helpful friends and medical professionals that I know to sit on our new board of directors and our professional advisory board."

"It sure sounds like you're off to a great start. What about permanent office space?"

"That's something I'd like to get your counsel on if you don't mind sharing some suggestions. Our group would really prefer not to spend our precious financial resources on rent and utilities, et cetera, so if you have any ideas, we'd be very grateful."

"I do have a few thoughts, but first, Tammy, can you tell me why launching your Healing Community is so important to you?"

Tammy smiles at me with a warmth and grace that stuns me as she confides, "I have cervical cancer. It's progressed. My doctor says that I'm responding well to the radiation and chemotherapy, but we both know that the outcome is likely pretty dire."

Her words hit me like a ton of bricks and words fail me. She smiles at me and consoles, "It's okay, Nathan, I know I have maybe three to five years left, and I want to do something meaningful with my remaining time so that others battling cancer and life-threatening diseases can come together to lean on each other and share their stories."

Tammy's frankness and personal warmth are so endearing that I say, "I admire you, your strength of character, your selflessness…I'll be happy to help however I can."

We spend the next hour talking about a lot of ideas. Our tablecloth is actually a white sheet of Kraft paper, and there's a cup containing colorful crayons, ostensibly for younger children to draw with during their meals. I use a crayon to jot down notes about different fundraising practices and suggestions, especially as they pertain to raising major gifts. By the end of our lunch the tablecloth is literally covered with words, phrases, names, and diagrams embellished in the most wonderful Crayola colors.

"Raising big money isn't rocket science. People give to people, so regardless of how important your Healing Community may be, you've got to remember that there are a lot of worthy charitable organizations out there vying for support. That's why it's so important to identify your prospects well and recruit people to join you on fundraising calls that the prospects know and respect and potentially owe."

"Remember, too, that money follows ideas and specific funding needs rather than general support. You mentioned your need for free or very low-cost office space, then you might consider approaching someone who has commercial real estate that's currently unoccupied. I have someone in mind who might be very sympathetic to your cause. I'll be happy to set up a meeting for the three of us if you're amenable."

Tammy reaches over and takes my hand. "You're a prince, Nathan, thank you so much. Just let me know when and where, and I'll be there. Can we please keep in touch in the future too? You've given me so many great ideas, and I can't wait to share them with our folks and move forward."

"Of course, anytime, Tammy! And, I have every expectation that you and your associates will be very successful."

As we stand up from the table, Tammy grabs the tablecloth with my colorful notes and says, "No way I'm leaving this baby behind!"

We say goodbye but keep in touch for a few years until I move away from Cincinnati to begin the new chapter in my life with Marlita. The most satisfying thing about my friendship with Tammy was that she actually employed many of the suggestions that I shared with her instead of merely nodding her head enthusiastically and promptly neglecting to follow up. That, plus the fact that under her leadership the Healing Community put together one of the most influential boards of directors I've ever seen, and the positive impact that organization had was monumental and truly helpful to hundreds of people fighting cancer.

It was a very sad day for me when I received a call from a friend in Cincinnati who had served on the Healing Community's board of directors informing me that Tammy had passed away. She was a woman of uncommon valor, a woman whose vision and energy were transcendent.

A few days after that I called Joe. "Hi there, did you know that Tammy Kaplan from the Healing Community recently passed away?"

"Yes, I saw her obituary in the *Enquirer*. She was quite a gal! Do you want me to prepare a check and make an appointment with their board president?"

"Yes, I do."

"How much do you want to give, Nathan?"

"Ask their board president how much they'd need to name the Healing Community's center in memory of Tammy in perpetuity."

"That's something they'll probably want to do anyway, Nathan."

"I understand, Joe. Please ask him anyway and prepare a check for whatever amount he says up to $3 million, then personally deliver it, okay? Tammy Kaplan deserves it…and so much more."

"Consider it done, my friend."

Chapter Fourteen

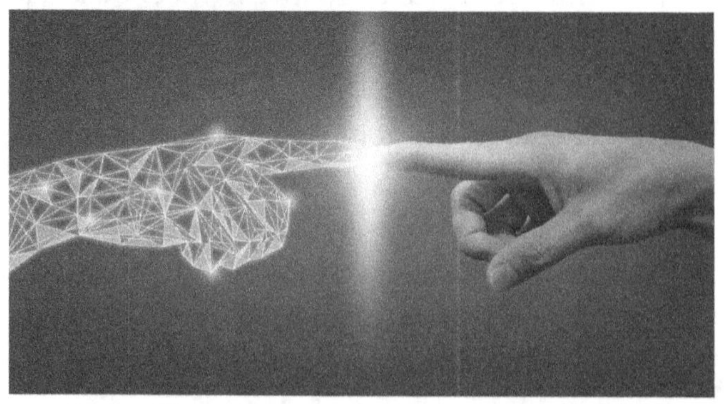

~ Travis and the Library ~

THE VERY MOMENT Travis Snyder enters the cool, quiet calm of the Putnam County Public Library, he feels like he can breathe easily again. This place is his sanctuary. His escape from home, from his parents who'd prefer that he was gone anyway. Travis will graduate from high school very soon and turn eighteen next month. He can't wait until he doesn't have to listen to the bickering or the smell of tobacco and alcohol from his stepfather. His parents aren't physically abusive toward each other or him, but it's a tough love in that house. He doesn't know how or why his mother puts up with him. She thinks her husband is basically a good man and believes he's going to need her because of his failing health. Life portends a hard road ahead, and Travis doesn't want to travel there.

In the library Travis feels safe and alive, amid volumes upon volumes covering every subject imaginable in a place of catalogued wonder. At first his visits to the library were for calmness and privacy, but he's developed a curiosity about not just the breadth of literature, but also how the librarians organize the collection. For the first time in his life he sees a possible career direction in library science and knows he'll have to continue his education if he wants to actualize that possibility. He researches the expense of a college education and blanches when he sees the costs of tuition. Even at a state community college, it'll take a lot more dough than he's got, and the thought of saddling himself with a huge amount of student debt is frightening to him.

After Travis finishes his homework, he slowly moseys down the rows of photography books. He's fascinated by the large volumes on astronomy and selects an exciting one with images taken by the James Webb Space Telescope. For Travis, it's the stuff that dreams are made of. He settles in a cozy chair by a window and begins slowly flipping one page after another reading photo captions and peering at the unfathomable. "Hmmm, maybe astronomy," he whispers to himself. "Wouldn't that be cool?" And again, his dreams are brought down to earth by the reality of the cost of a college education. Time flies by, and Travis is surprised by Matt Matlock, the library director, who says, "We're about to close, young fella, would you like to check out that book and take it home?"

"Oh, sorry! I guess I lost track of time."

The director laughs and says, "Yeah, that's one of the beauties of coming to the library. Are you thinking about going to college for astronomy?"

"Uh, not sure, sir, I've been thinking about maybe a degree in library science, but astronomy is so cool too. Unfortunately, I'd need to find a job this summer to make some money to start school if I can even get accepted somewhere."

"Well, I've noticed you here a lot over the past few months. We don't pay great, but if you're interested, I think we could use a bright guy to work at the reference desk. You interested?"

"Heck yeah, that would be great. Whatever you'll pay will be more than I'm making as a student, and I could start whenever you want!"

"Tomorrow's Saturday. You want to meet me here around ten o'clock, and we'll get you officially on staff and started at the reference desk? How's that sound?"

"I'll be here for sure…and thank you so much!"

"Great, now scoot on out of here. I'm tired and hungry and want to grab some dinner, then crash. Been a long day!"

Travis shakes Mr. Matlock's hand and heads for the door. He watches him exit the building and recalls being about the young man's age, and the struggles he felt deciding about college and which career path to follow.

The days that follow see Travis Snyder become a regular fixture at the library. He graduates from high school and continues to live at home so he can save money for school. He's not at home very much, so he manages to overlook his stultifying home life.

Matt Matlock keeps an eye on Travis's work habits and asks a veteran coworker to help guide him along and even do some online research with him about colleges and scholarships. Travis learns very quickly and has a very positive attitude working with visitors.

One evening after work Matt decides to have dinner at the Monon Diner instead of preparing and eating a meal by himself. He's eaten there often over the years even way before Stella Chastain took over ownership.

"Evening, Matt, how're things in the library biz?" Stella asks as she leads him over to a booth.

"Good," he replies. "The work is never-ending, of course, but I like staying busy."

"How's your staff doing? I always find it's hard to hire good people, and harder still to keep them."

"Yeah, people are the best and the worst part of the job, I guess, but we've got some very good employees. I hired a young fella recently who just graduated from Greencastle High School, and he's been terrific. He wants to start college this fall, but he really can't afford it, and I think his parents are on the borderline of making too much money for him to qualify for a lot of scholarships. He also doesn't want to rely on them and is frightened about carrying a lot of student debt. He's a great, smart kid who wants to go to school, and I fear it's a dream he may have to postpone for a long time until he's got the resources to do it on his own."

Stella listens closely and says, "So, you feel like this young man is worth, uh, investing in?"

"I sure do. There's a limit to how much I can pay him because he doesn't have a college degree, and I'd probably have a riot among the staff if they found out I was paying him above his pay grade. Regardless, I wish I had a way to ease his transition into adult life. As you know, it can be a very daunting challenge."

"Do you have any idea how much it would cost him to attend a four-year state school like Indiana University, including room and board and other living expenses?"

"Yeah, probably around $30,000 per year before any student aid…about $12,000 for tuition and another $16,000 or more for books and on-campus room and board."

"So, you figure about $120,000 for four years?"

"Yeah, about that, maybe more. And, if you go to graduate school, the costs just keep adding on. It's a lot of dough for Travis, and I understand that his stepfather's health is deteriorating rapidly due to some poor lifestyle choices. And, his mom stays at home looking after her husband, so she's got no real income. They're between a rock and a hard place."

"I understand. Would you mind if I did a little looking around to see if I can come up with some ways to help him financially?"

"No, Stella, that would be great. I've pretty much exhausted my sources. I believe in this kid, and it would be wonderful to help get him started in life."

"Why don't you stop by for dinner, say the beginning of next week and maybe bring Travis along. I may have something to suggest. Give me a call first to let me know when you might be coming, okay?"

After Matt Matlock leaves, Stella picks up her phone and calls Nathan.

"Hi Nathan, hope I'm not catching you at a bad time."

"No, I'm good, Stella. Just doing some writing while the spirit moves me, but I can use a break. What's up?"

"You know Matt Matlock, right?"

"Our library director? Sure! Matt and I have met several times when the library buys my novels to put into their circulation, or to host an author talk for me. Good man! I respect him. What about him?"

"Matt was just here for dinner, and we got to talking about a young man named Travis Snyder who recently graduated from high school and wants to go to college either to be a librarian or an astronomer. Matt has hired him at the library, but we both know that doesn't pay much. Anyway, Matt says the lad comes from a challenged family and really feels like this young man could use a break. Apparently, they've looked into several scholarship possibilities which don't seem to be especially promising, so I'm calling you to see what you think."

"What about taking out a student loan?"

"Matt says young Travis doesn't want to take on a major debt because he feels like he'll really be behind the eight ball financially for years, plus his mom's gonna need some help if and when his stepdad dies."

"Well, I sure can't blame Travis for not wanting to take on a lot of debt. I don't know where we went wrong in this country by saddling so many young people with mountains of debt from student loans. It's tantamount to having a mortgage without owning a home. It's nuts!"

"Matt figures Travis would need about $30,000 a year to go to school and live. What do you think about giving that amount to him and offering a full four-year ride if he keeps his grades up and proves himself?"

"I'm comfortable with that, Stella. My dad was a full-time college professor at the University of Cincinnati, so I was able to go to college tuition-free, so yeah, I got off really easy with college expenses. So, from the way you describe Travis and his situation at home, I'm okay with it if you and Matt are."

"I haven't said anything to Matt about this as a possibility, and rest assured I'd never mention your name. I told him I might have an idea for them and asked him to drop by the diner next week and bring Travis along. That's where we stand."

"I like the suggestion, Stella. I'll give Joe a call when we hang up and ask him to send you a check tomorrow in Travis Snyder's name for $40,000 and another check in the amount of $25,000, payable to the library, because Matt's being such a good samaritan. No doubt, the library can always use the dough."

"That's very generous of you, Nathan. Thank you so much, and please send my best wishes to Joe. I'll let you know how it all unfolds."

Five days fly by, and Stella receives a phone call from Matt Matlock saying that he and Travis would like to drop by the Monon for dinner around seven o'clock. Stella confirms that would be perfect.

As they enter the diner Stella quickly sizes up young Mr. Snyder, and her gut tells her that Matt's judgment was probably very accurate.

"Good evening, gentlemen! I'm Stella Chastain, Travis. I own the Monon, and I'm delighted you and Mr. Matlock have joined us for dinner this evening.

Your meals are on the house so please help yourself to whatever you want."

"That's mighty generous of you, Stella, but I'd be happy to pay for us."

"Let's agree to argue about the tab at the end of your dinner, okay, Matt?"

The two men have a seat, and Stella takes care of making sure everything is running smoothly for her customers. Before long, the diner clears out, and Stella joins the men at their table.

"Had enough to eat, young fella?" she asks Travis.

"Yeah, that was great." Matt concurs.

"So, Travis, Mr. Matlock was in here one day last week talking about how you're doing a fine job at the library and thinking seriously about going to college this fall."

"Yes, ma'am, I've even had an interview with the admissions office at IU, and the lady I met with seems to think I should be able to get accepted."

"That sounds terrific!"

"Yeah, but I don't have the money for tuition, and my stepdad's in a real bad way physically, so I don't know…"

Stella looks at Matt and then at Travis. "What if I knew a source that would pay for your freshman year, including tuition, books, on-campus lodging and living expenses."

"That would be great, Ms. Chastain, but I don't know how I'd ever be able to repay that."

Stella pulls out an envelope and hands it to Travis. He opens it and sees a cashier's check in his name in the amount of $40,000. His eyes go wide and his mouth goes open in shock. Matt sees the check, and his reaction is virtually the same.

"But, I don't understand, Ms. Chastain!"

"I have a friend who's very well-off financially. I told him about my conversation with Mr. Matlock who's been a real champion for you, and this money is for you to spend for your first year in college. I'm not at liberty to say your benefactor's name, but he told me to advise you that he'll pay for all four years of your college plus living expenses provided you stay in school and make good grades. Is it a deal?"

Matt and Travis look at each other in stunned delight. "Heck yeah, it's a deal! I can't believe this."

"There's another condition that goes along with this. We don't want you breathing a word about this, even to your parents, and I'd like to ask Matt here to help you open a bank account and follow through with your application to Indiana University. Are you both comfortable with that?"

Both nod their heads affirmatively. "Oh, Stella, this is amazing. I don't know how we can ever thank you enough. Right, Travis?"

Travis has tears in his eyes. "No one has ever been this kind to me, ever! I promise to not let any of you down."

"There's one last thing, Matt. Because you and the library have displayed such unconditional support, we want you to have this." She hands Matt another envelope, and he sees a second cashier's check, made payable to the Putnam County Public Library, in the amount of $25,000. He's shocked again.

"Oh, Stella, I don't know who your generous friend is, but will you please extend our deepest thanks to him? This is all so wonderful!"

The three of them chat a bit longer, and then get up from the table. Matt drops thirty dollars on the table. "Please! No arguments, Stella, this is the very least we can do, and I promise to keep this all confidential, and to keep you apprised of this fine young man's progress."

There are hugs all around, and then they part company.

After they leave Stella calls her benefactor and informs him, "Mission accomplished, Nathan! I think this was a very good deed. Thank you! I'll keep you posted on how Travis does."

"Great! Glad it worked out so well. I'll let Joe know. I'm sure he'd enjoy hearing from you too."

Chapter Fifteen

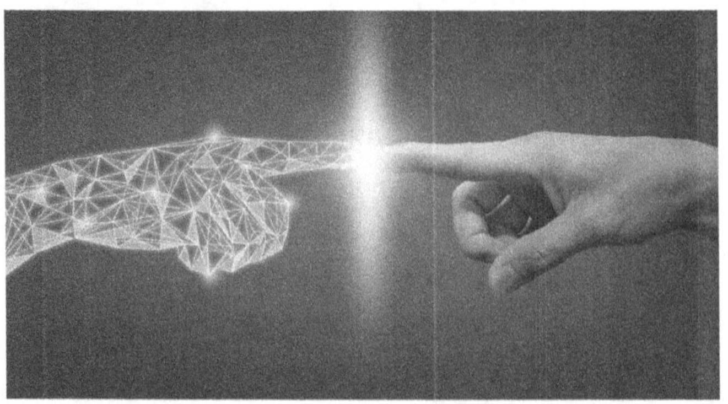

As I sit here at my desk and write each new chapter of *Given Names*, thoughts of other people and organizations I think about helping come to my mind: People that I know, the work that they do, and the impact they have on our community, or very simply, good folks who are trying hard at living a decent life and could still use a boost. I close my eyes and envision a scene, and immediately I know where I want my writing to go next.

~ Asbury Chapel ~
and
Greencastle Summer Music Festival

The lone figure sits in a shadowed alcove in Asbury Chapel. He's clothed in a long black robe with a simple, braided sash around his waist and a crucifix hanging around his neck to his sternum. The only color that's visible is a shock of his reddish-blond hair. He leans forward in deep personal contemplation, looking monk-like in his attire bathed in a very subtle Rembrandt-like light. The sound of silence enshrouds him, and he is alone with the beating of his heart and his God. Then, from near the sanctuary, Reverend Langston Bryant suddenly hears a most soulful sound. *Ave Maria* performed by Professor Enrique Bergman on cello. The rich sounds created by each stroke of Professor Bergman's bow imbues the chapel with a wondrous solemnity, and Reverend Bryant dips even deeper into his spiritual thoughts.

From there, Enrique follows with one of Bach's Church Contatas, and then another and another, and the good reverend finally rises from his quiet contemplation and walks toward the sanctuary to greet his long-time friend Enrique.

"Oh, I didn't see you there, Langston, have you been here long?"

"Yes, Enrique, I decided that I could use some alone time with my Creator, so I was sitting in the alcove in the shadows. Your music was truly inspirational. Heavenly, actually! Thank you!"

"You're very welcome. I'm pleased you enjoyed. Well, you know we have our opening concert coming up this Wednesday evening for the Greencastle Summer Music Festival, and I wanted to practice a couple of pieces that I haven't played for a while. I can't believe that this is the start of our nineteenth concert season. Hard to believe how far we've come."

"That's wonderful, and yes, of course, I'll be in the audience applauding loudly!"

"So, how are things here at church? No doubt, you're conducting inspirational services and sermons, profound Bible studies, and important outreach programs."

"Well, I'll leave it to my parishioners to say whether my services and sermons are inspirational or not. We can always do more as a community of faith. I sure know that I try, but there's always an opportunity to live our faith more fully. And then, there are the mundane things that demand attention and money like the water damage to the plaster near the ceiling and a few other annoyances. It's a real balancing act, and we're gonna need to raise some money somehow to keep our beloved chapel in good shape physically and also be in a position financially to meet the spiritual expectations of our congregation. I'm not sure how we're going to raise the money that we need to do it all, but with God's help, I'm hopeful we'll find a way."

"I have faith in you, Langston. Perhaps I should make an appeal for contributions to both Asbury Chapel and the Summer Music Festival during the intermission at Wednesday's concert. Lord knows, both of our organizations can use the money, and Asbury has been the home of our summer music festival for nearly two decades now."

"I'll leave that to your good judgment, Enrique. In the meantime, my friend, I would love to hear more of your divine cello music."

Wednesday evening arrives, and Marlita and I are scurrying around trying to get out the door and go to Asbury Chapel. Tonight's program will be a musical revue featuring Enrique on cello and a host of mostly local musicians that many of us have heard before, and we always come away aching for more.

"Hey, are you about ready?!" I holler up to Marlita who's finishing getting dressed.

"Five more minutes. Don't worry, you're not going to miss anything. Enrique always enjoys making his announcements prior to the music."

"I'll go warm up Pappy. Take your time…but speed it up a little, will ya please?!" That's just an example of the mixed messages Marlita claims I send frequently. Like I've said, "I'm not a perfect person."

The traffic in town at seven o'clock on a Wednesday evening during the summer is light, and there's always abundant, free parking available in Asbury Chapel's lot. We arrive on time and walk through the front entrance. We've been coming to the concert series for so many years now, we recognize and wave to several folks we know as we finally decide on a row to settle in. We both grab seat cushions to ensure more comfort than sitting on the rigid wooden pew.

A few minutes past 7:30 p.m., Professor Enrique Bergman approaches the podium and introduces himself as the founder and artistic director of our great festival. Enrique and I have known each other a long time, and we've worked closely together in the past. Fact is, I was the first president of the festival's board of directors and helped raise endowment funds to provide steady but modest income. I have the greatest respect for Enrique because he's a cellist and teacher par excellence and also a very talented promoter and raconteur. This man can work a room with the best of 'em!

"Welcome, everyone, for the opening of our nineteenth concert season. We have a variety of musical treats for you this evening, and a special message I want to share with you during the intermission, so I hope you'll sit back and enjoy our musical revue, and I'll be back with you shortly."

Marlita and I do as Enrique suggests and get comfortable and listen as long-time music icon, Claude Cymerman, delights with his impeccable performances of Gershwin favorites on piano, followed by wondrous improv by the amazing Cathie Malach. Then, there's a brief break as Ming-Hui Kuo sets up her marimba and takes the audience on a magical mystery tour of sound and vibrations. It's a stunning set of performances leaving the audience enthralled by the talent that Enrique has brought on stage. After Ming's music leaves everyone nearly breathless, it's time for the brief intermission.

"Weren't they all just fantastic?!" Enrique exhorts. "And, I know you're not going to want to leave early because coming up during the second half are blues legend, Tad Robinson, and his world-famous band. But, before we bring Tad and company on stage, I want to take a few minutes to ask your help with something very important."

"As you know, Asbury Chapel has been our home since the beginning, and thankfully, we've never been asked to pay any money for 'rent' in this inspirational place. We've also been blessed by other organizations in town, as well, like the Inn-at-Asbury which provides free lodging for our out-of-town performers, but tonight I want to focus on Asbury."

"As you know we've never charged admission and exist solely through donations from friends like you, a few grants, and income from our endowment fund at the Putnam County Community Foundation. As you look around you'll notice that the ceilings and walls in the sanctuary and nave are in need of repair, and I'm asking each of you to consider making a special contribution to Asbury's capital fund drive. I know, I can already see some of you squirming in your seats at the talk of giving money, but I want to reiterate my personal gratitude to Asbury's congregation by making my own pledge of charitable support.

"Our board members Steve and Linda will distribute some gift envelopes for Asbury's Covenant Campaign, and I hope you'll be as generous as your pocketbook and spirit of giving permit. Thank you very much!"

A few minutes pass as gift envelopes are distributed among the rows, and I notice several people in the audience nodding their heads positively as their envelopes reach them. Marlita and I look at each other and nod as well. "I'll speak with Enrique after the concert."

"And now, ladies and gentlemen, without further delay, please welcome Mister Tad Robinson and his band!"

From the very first note, Tad and his guys light up the room with soulful music and style…guitar, drums, keyboard, and The Man himself wailing away on harmonica and bringing us all back down to earth with his soothing voice. There are two cover tunes, but most of the selections were new songs composed by my pal TR.

"Whew! Quite a night!" Marlita gushes. "It's so great that even as a classical musician, Enrique encourages all genres of music."

"Yeah, I remember Enrique quoting someone to me, 'That there are only two types of music…good music and bad music.' Might've been Yo-Yo Ma."

As people begin to leave the concert, Marlita and I walk to the front of the sanctuary to exchange salutations with the musicians, and then I pull Enrique aside and motion for Reverend Bryant to join us. "I realize this isn't the best time for a discussion about your fundraising needs, but I want to be helpful to both of your causes. I believe I know someone who might be in a position to help. Would you both be available for a meeting with this person, say, this coming Friday?"

"Well, as you can imagine, when I'm called upon to help my congregants, I need to always make that my priority. I believe Friday, say around four o'clock should work, though. How about you, Enrique?"

I look at Enrique and interject before he can reply, "Whatever you've got scheduled, reschedule it!"

Enrique looks at me curiously and sees the sincerity in my eyes. He recognizes that this is a *command performance.*

"Why yes, of course, Friday at four, it is!"

Two days later at one minute before four o'clock a silver Audi pulls into Asbury Chapel's parking lot, and Joe Daniels gets out and stretches his legs after the 165-mile drive from Cincinnati. He looks at the chapel's fine Tudor architecture and understands the need to keep it in good repair. He walks up the steps and enters Asbury's solemn calm. He sees two men talking by the altar and approaches them. One is dressed in a minister's robe and the other is clad in a tweed jacket and dark slacks.

"From your attire I surmise that you are Reverend Langston Bryant and you, sir, are Professor Enrique Bergman. I'm Joseph Daniels, an attorney with Hoffman Fabian and True in Cincinnati."

"Very nice to meet you," Langston and Enrique say in near-unison. "We take it that you're the gentleman that Nathan Andrews said would be meeting with us today."

"I am. Nathan knows that I represent a very wealthy client who might be interested in supporting Asbury Chapel's building needs. I've discussed this with my client who wishes to remain anonymous, and he's agreed for me to meet with you today." Joe pulls an envelope out of his briefcase and hands it to Reverend Bryant. "My client is pleased to make this gift, and hopes that it may motivate others to contribute as well. He prefers that you use it as a challenge-grant, matching each dollar contributed by others, but he does not wish to tie your hands with strict rules, so you may use it as you see fit."

The good reverend's eyes go wide with wonder as he sees a check made payable to Asbury Chapel in the amount of $1 million.

"I realize that this amount may be more than you expected, but my client has every faith that whatever dollars you don't require for building maintenance will be put to very good use."

Langston smiles and stammers, "It's one of the few times in my life that I'm totally speechless. This is a miracle. Can we please thank the person who made this gift possible? The check mentions a trust's name but not the name of our benefactor."

"Right," Joe confirms. "And, while this may be frustrating for you, my client wishes to remain anonymous."

The reverend looks heavenward and whispers the words: "Thank you, whoever you are!"

"And you, Professor Bergman, my client wishes to acknowledge your career as the artistic director of the Greencastle Summer Music Festival. Mr. Andrews and my client are very close friends, and upon his suggestion, your benefactor didn't hesitate to have me prepare this check for you as well."

He hands an envelope to Enrique who opens it. "Seriously? This is for the Summer Music Festival? It's for a half-million dollars! Seriously?!"

"Quite so, Professor! Please use it as you wish. Our only proviso with these gifts is that you please not badger Nathan Andrews about who your benefactor is because I can assure you that he will not violate that confidence. Are we in agreement about this?"

"Yes, but may we at least thank Nathan for recommending us to your client? I think we'd both feel awkward not saying something to him."

"Yes, that's perfectly fine, but please resist the urge to go beyond that. Like I said, Nathan won't violate his friend's expressed wishes."

Langston and Enrique nod their heads in giddy agreement. Joe shakes hands with each man, picks up his briefcase, waves goodbye, and walks out of the quiet calm of Asbury Chapel. As he approaches his car, Joe can hear animated voices coming from within the chapel, and once inside his Audi, he picks up his cell phone and dials a number. "Everything went as you'd hoped. They're both pretty tickled with the surprises. I'm leaving now and should be at your place in about fifteen minutes."

"Or, would you prefer meeting Marlita and me at the Monon instead? I realize it's still early for dinner, but we could sit outside at Stella's new patio and have a few libations first. I know Marlita would prefer being outside on such a beautiful evening, and we'd have a great view of that lovely caboose."

"I'm not sure whose 'caboose' you're thinking of, but it sounds like a great plan to me! I'll see you there."

Chapter Sixteen

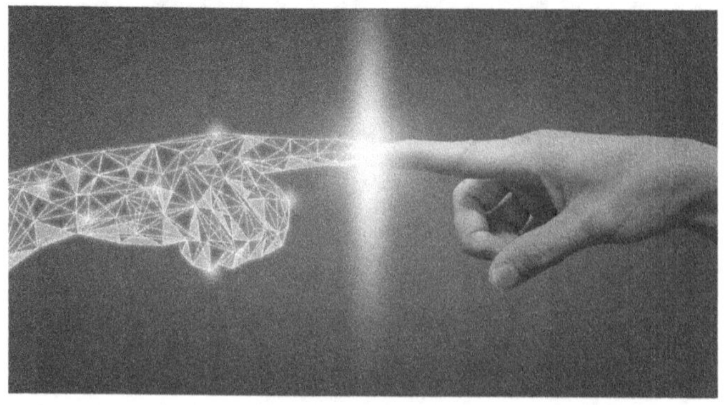

WHEN MARLITA AND I ARRIVE at the Monon, we see that Joe has already been seated outside. I park Pappy near the J.J. Hunter caboose, and Marlita and I join Joe at his table. A young waitress named Jackie comes and takes our drink orders, and I ask her: "Is Stella not here tonight? She ordinarily welcomes most people as they enter."

"No, I got a phone call from Aunt Stella a few hours ago saying that she wasn't feeling well and asking if I could fill in for her tonight. So, here I am."

"Did she say if she had a stomach flu or something?" Joe asks with concern.

"I don't know for sure. She just said that she was feeling pretty beat up and wouldn't be in today which is unusual for Aunt Stella because, unless she's really contagious with some bug, she always comes to work."

Jackie takes our drink orders, and Joe and I look at each other skeptically. "While I was waiting for you guys to arrive, I received a text message from Josh, the manager at Old American Bank, asking me to contact him. His message was a little cryptic, but he said that there's an issue with the check we'd given to the animal shelter."

"Seriously?!" I ask. "Did he say what kind of problem in his message?"

"I just got the message as you guys were parking Pappy, so I haven't had a chance to get back to him yet."

"Let's give him a call. I'll bet he's still at the bank."

Joe and I get up and walk several feet away so we have some privacy, and Joe places the call.

"Hello, this is Josh Tellerman, how may I help you?"

"Josh, this is Joe Daniels getting back to you. I just got your message about there being a problem with our check to the animal shelter. What's going on?"

"Uh, yeah, yesterday morning shortly after we opened the bank this fellow comes in wearing a sheriff's uniform asking us to deposit this large check he brought with him, and then to transfer it to a separate, personal account."

"And?" Joe asks.

"It was a check for $1 million, made payable to the Putnam County Animal Shelter. Guy named Snurd claimed to be the county's animal control officer and said he was asked by his supervisor to deposit the check."

Joe's *bullshit detector* immediately goes into high alert, as he recalls the brusque treatment that he and Stella received when they went to the shelter a few days ago to meet with Gus Miles and deliver the check.

"So, what tipped you off that this was weird?"

"Well, we don't get checks like that very often, like never, so that got my attention. Plus, there was a stamped area on the back of the check reading, 'For deposit only. Putnam County Animal Shelter.' It looked rather crude, like it was handmade. It just didn't look right. And, then when this Snurd guy wanted to immediately transfer the million dollars to a personal account with his name on it, my gut told me this was nefarious."

"What'd you say to him?"

"I told him that I'd need a little more documentation in order to proceed with the deposit, and he didn't like that. He got petulant and said he was there on official business. I apologized to him, but he got huffy and stormed off."

"So, what did you do next?" Joe asks.

"I know Sheriff Seta very well so I called him for verification about the check and confirmation that Officer Snurd was, in fact, an officer in the sheriff's department.

"And?"

"Sheriff Seta didn't have a clue what I was talking about and said he'd look into it and get back to me which he did about an hour later."

"And?!" Joe prompts.

"So, apparently this Officer Snurd has been a regular pain in the butt for the department, and Sheriff Seta shipped him off to the animal shelter to be the county's animal control officer. I think he just wanted to get this guy out of sight some place like the shelter where he wouldn't be a problem. He then informed me that Snurd had apparently phoned the department a little while ago saying he quit without giving any formal written notice or a reason for his resignation. All pretty wonky!"

"I'll say it is," Joe replies. "Well, thank you very much for using your great instincts about this. Clearly, Officer Snurd isn't the sharpest dude. When we hang up, I'll contact our trust's bank instructing them to cancel payment on any attempt to cash this check. I'll have them prepare a new check for the animal shelter and won't make the mistake of leaving it with anyone other than the shelter's director. I really appreciate your contacting me directly."

"You're very welcome. I knew that you were the contact person on other checks the trust has made to local charities, so you were the person that I knew to call."

"Thanks, Mr. Tellerman, you did the right thing." They hang up.

"So, Nathan, I think you could hear our conversation. What do you want to do aside from my canceling payment on the check?"

"From what you've told me about your and Stella's treatment by this Snurd feller at the shelter and what Josh Tellerman just related to you, I'm thinking that maybe we should make sure that Stella's okay."

Joe nods his agreement. Jackie brings our dinners to us, and I tell Marlita what's going on with the shelter's money. "Joe and I want to drive over to Stella's and make sure she's all right. Do you mind if we take off?"

"No, not at all. I can have Jackie put your dinners in a to-go box and drive Pappy back home. Yeah, please go check on Stella."

Joe and I climb into his Audi, and I give him directions to Stella's home. When we get there all of the lights are out. I try reaching her on her cell phone, but a recording immediately asks us to leave a message.

We lightly knock on her door, but there's no reply. We knock again, and then again, she doesn't come to the door.

"Let's go around back and see if her car's there. Maybe she had to go to the drugstore or something."

"Or, maybe she's in the kitchen or bathroom and just didn't hear us knock."

We walk around to the rear of the house and see her car parked in the garage. "Well, she should be home."

We step up to the back porch, and I knock on the door. There's no answer at first, so I knock again. A few moments later we vaguely see Stella's face appear through a lace window curtain. Then, she opens the door, but what we see isn't Stella's pretty face. She's battered and bruised and puffy looking. Definitely not stomach flu. Her lip is split, and she has a nasty looking black eye. Her petite nose is battered, and she has a jagged gash on her forehead. We're horrified by the shape she's in.

"I was gonna call you but just couldn't manage to do it right away."

We enter her house, and Joe gently gives Stella a soft embrace. "What happened? Do we need to take you to the emergency room?"

"No, I think I'll be all right in a couple of days. I didn't want you guys to see me like this."

"What happened, Stella?" Joe repeats.

"That turd Snurd happened! He showed up here all pissed off because the bank apparently wouldn't deposit the check we brought to the shelter. Somehow he must've gotten it before that gal could put it in the safe. Snurd wanted me to contact the bank to say it was okay to deposit the check, and when I refused and told him to get the hell away from my house, he started getting rough."

I say, "I'm calling the police to report this assault, and then I'd like it if you'd please come to our place where you'll be safe, and we can look after you."

Stella is reluctant to leave at first, and Joe finally convinces her it's the right thing to do. We take a few minutes for Stella to change clothes and collect a few things for her stay with us.

When we get in Joe's Audi, Stella says through a crooked smile: "I guess I'm earning my retainer, guys."

Joe and I are both seething with anger. "I'm so sorry, Stella," I say. "I never would've dreamed in a million years that something like this could happen."

"And, that's why anonymity for you and Marlita is so important, Nathan. I swear, Stella, this Snurd prick is going to pay a very hefty price for hurting you and trying to steal the shelter's money."

I've never seen Joe Daniels so furious in my life.

Chapter Seventeen

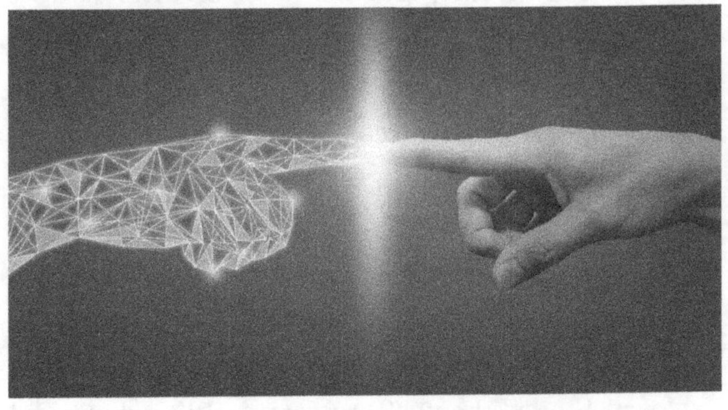

S TELLA DECIDES TO STAY WITH US for only two days and then insists she needs to get back to work. Her split lip is healing thanks to applications of Neosporin, and the bruising on her face has faded to a pale yellow and green, most of which she's able to cover with makeup. Most people would be gun shy after getting physically assaulted, but if any-thing, Stella is showing even more moxie. Joe feels very protective of her, but says he has to get back to

Cincinnati as well and offers to drive Stella home so she can get her car. After they leave our house, Marlita and I sit on our porch swing talking about the hateful things some people will do for money.

"I guess sometimes no good deed goes unpunished, huh?" she says as we hold each other.

"Joe was right that we should try our best to maintain our anonymity. I can't bear the thought of anything ever happening to you, Marlita. The sheriff's department has an APB out to apprehend Snurd, but my guess is that he's long gone by now. Hope so. I still want us to give the money to the animal shelter, but this time we'll make certain that Mr. Miles is on duty. I've been thinking of making the gift as a memorial gift, but I need to talk with Gus Miles about it first. It could be a sweet surprise for an old friend."

"Someone I know?" she asks.

"Yes, but I'd like it to be a surprise for you too."

"Okay…this is a little intriguing…"

"Good! I still want it to be a surprise."

We agree to continue to stay positive and begin thinking about who else we might want to support.

~ Jenny and Ellie ~
Transcend

"You know, Nathan, there's someone I've been thinking about, and I wanted to get your opinion."

"Oh, who's that?"

"One of my yoga students, Jenny. She's been coming to classes for a while now, but she's very quiet and often leaves immediately after class is over. I'm not sure if you've ever met her."

"I think I've heard you mention her name, but I can't put a face on her. What's unique about her?"

"Well, for the longest time I didn't know much about Jenny because she's very private, and she exudes a deep personal sadness. Recently though she's opened up to me more about her personal life, and I've learned that she's been dealing with some very serious family trauma. My impression is that she's had to become very strong emotionally because of an accident that changed her and her daughter's lives. This past Tuesday evening Jenny uncharacteristically stayed after class and asked if we could talk. Of course, I agreed, and when she began it was like a floodgate had been opened and years of private pain came pouring out."

Jenny began, "Carl, Ellie, and I were driving along Manhattan Road three years ago near the old Antioch church. We were taking Ellie to a music lesson in Greencastle, and Carl and I were gonna do some grocery shopping while Ellie was with her teacher. It was a gray, rainy day. It was getting dark, and the roads were slick, but not awful. As we rounded a sharp curve a grain truck pulled out in front of us, and we slammed into it. Carl did his best to maintain control, but our car skidded off the road, flipped over, and we landed pinned up against a fallen tree. It happened so quickly that there was nothing that Carl could do."

"The driver of the grain truck immediately came running to our aid and called 911 when he saw how serious the accident was. It wasn't his fault really. Just one of those freak accidents, I guess, but Carl died upon impact, and Ellie and I were trapped inside our car until the EMTs finally arrived. I was very banged up, but Ellie was in worse shape. She couldn't move her legs. We were both airlifted to the

ER in Danville, and once we were stabilized, they transported us to St. Francis Hospital in Greenwood. I had a ruptured spleen and neck and head injuries, but poor Ellie lost the use of her legs."

"Oh, my God! That's horrible, Marlita. How're they faring now?"

"I didn't want to press Jenny for too many details because she's so private, but she says that after many months of grieving Carl's death and learning how to deal with a teenage paraplegic daughter that they're managing to get on with life. Honestly, Nathan, I don't think they've got much money. To his credit, the owner of the grain truck company gave Jenny some money. He didn't need to do it because his driver wasn't found at fault, but it's not nearly enough to cover ongoing medical expenses and the cost of living. Very heartbreaking."

"Jeez, I'll say."

"Jenny went on to tell me that despite her life-changing injuries, Ellie is doing well in the eighth grade and even talks about going to college when she graduates. She just started a new school program called Transcend that enrolls eligible students like Ellie to complete readiness requirements and participate in weekly mentoring. The desired outcome is to empower each student to be a self-sufficient adult and a leader in their community, basically living a life of purpose, boldness, and impact."

"Wow, I've heard of the Transcend program, Marlita, but because we don't have school-age children, I've never known anyone who actually went through the program. If you feel strongly that this is something important, I'm with you in offering our support. Why don't I ask Joe to identify the contact person for Transcend and prepare a check.

"That would be great, Nathan. I recall Jenny telling me that the codirectors of the Transcend program are a couple named Hunter and Lydia Vickman. Joe shouldn't have any trouble tracking them down through Ellie's school. I'm thinking a half-million dollar grant would go a long way."

"Okay, that's very doable. How much do you think we should give to Jenny and Ellie?"

"I'm not rightly sure, Nathan. Are you comfortable having Stella deliver a check to them for a million dollars? I know that Jenny's a very proud woman, but I think she'd be relieved to have a very nice nest egg. I don't want her to think that she got the money as a result of our conversations though."

"I don't think maintaining our anonymity will be a problem, Marlita. Stella's very good at covering our tracks. Let's do it."

A week later Joe Daniels arrives back in Greencastle at my request. He'd tracked down the Vickmans through the Transcend program's website and arranged a meeting with Hunter at the library on the guise of wanting to volunteer as a mentor in the Transcend program.

"It's very nice to meet you, Mr. Daniels, and I'm delighted that you wish to volunteer in our program. If you don't mind I have some questions for you to make certain you're a good fit for our students. Since we're talking about juveniles, I'm sure you understand."

"Yes, of course, Mr. Vickman, I totally get it. Actually though, I must confess that I haven't been entirely up-front with you about my motivation for this meeting."

Hunter has a look of concern on his face. "Uh, I don't quite understand."

"I'm actually an attorney with the law firm of Hoffman Fabian and True in Cincinnati, and I've arranged this meeting with you at the request of a client."

"Again, I don't quite understand, Mr. Daniels. Is there a problem that I'm unaware of with our Transcend program?"

Joe smiles and says, "My client and I have done some research of Transcend's efficacy in helping to prepare young students for postsecondary education, and the only problem we see is that there aren't even more students enrolled."

Hunter relaxes a bit. "And, who is your client, and what exactly are your intentions?"

"My client is someone who wishes to remain anonymous, but he asked me to give this to you." Joe pulls out an envelope and hands it to a rather bewildered Hunter Vickman.

"Half a million dollars?! Is this for real?"

"It is, indeed, and my client wishes to congratulate you for working with local families and school administrations in making this important program available. The money is for the Transcend program to use however you feel will be most helpful."

Hunter sits in stunned silence.

"Through my research into your program, I've also learned that you and your wife have already contributed quite a large sum of money to advance your mission. My client and I are impressed by your personal generosity, all the more reason that we don't want you to feel alone in your mission."

"Well, you're very kind to say that, and I'm not sure where you get your information because my wife and I have also endeavored to keep our philanthropy private, but we are most grateful for your client's help. It'll certainly go a long way for the kids. Please thank him for us."

"It's our pleasure…and thank you for living your faith."

After a few moments, Joe looks at his watch, and says, "Please excuse me, Mr. Vickman, but I've got to move along. Duty calls, as you know." He shakes Hunter's hand, collects his belongings, and contentedly walks out the door and into the afternoon sunlight.

"Ellie! C'mon and give me a hand. It's almost time for dinner, sweetie! Would you please set the table?"

"Okay, be there in a minute, Mom!" Ellie guides her wheelchair from the den into the kitchen and watches her mom stir a large pot of soup on the stovetop.

"What're you working on...a homework assignment?"

"I finished my homework already and was working on a questionnaire for the Transcend program."

"Are you enjoying the program?"

"Yeah, the huddles are interesting because we talk about different school topics and some ethics issues with our mentors too."

"So, what courses are you most interested in?

"Uh, I like the science courses, especially biology, the most."

"Do you think you might like to be a vet or teach that in school?"

"Maybe, but I was thinking it could be way cool to be a doctor!"

"Hmm, that would be cool, but a lot of hard work, and it would take a lot of money to go to medical school."

"I know, but I'm only in the eighth grade, so it's not like I need to make my mind up tomorrow."

"True, but I'm proud of you for having a direction you're leaning toward."

"Yeah, that's one of the best parts about the Transcend huddles. Our small group of students can think out loud about our goals, and our mentors help give us encouragement about following our dreams and being of service to others."

After dinner Jenny washes the dishes, and Ellie dries them and puts them away. Despite losing the use of her legs, she's done a very good job in adapting her lifestyle to be productive around the house. Jenny always keeps a watchful eye on her handicapped daughter and still has to help her with some things, but Ellie has become very self-sufficient.

It's about eight o'clock, and they've just settled in to watch some some television when they hear the doorbell ring. "Hmm, I wonder who that could be. I wasn't expecting anyone, were you, Ellie?"

"No, Cindy said she might stop by to watch TV with us, but I think she would've texted me to say she was coming. Jenny walks to the door and peers through the peep hole. She sees a vaguely familiar woman's face and opens the door about four inches wide. "Can I help you?"

"Good evening, Jenny, my name's Stella Chastain. I don't believe we've ever met, but I was hoping to have a word with you and Ellie."

Jenny remains cordial but says, "What do you want to talk about? If you're selling something, I just don't believe we're interested. Thank you very much." She starts to close the front door.

"Jenny, I'm not here to sell you anything. I've been asked to stop by and speak with you about something very important though."

Jenny sizes Stella up and says, "Okay, but we're about to watch our program, so if this won't take too long, you're welcome to come in for a few minutes."

Ellie wheels her chair into the entry hall, and Stella introduces herself. The three of them have a seat in the living room, and Stella begins.

"First off, I want to reiterate I'm not here to sell you anything. Like I said, my name's Stella Chastain, and I own the Monon Diner."

"Oh yes, that's where I know you from. I knew I'd seen you somewhere."

"I'll try to be brief," Stella replies. "I've been asked by someone who's taken a special interest in you and your daughter to deliver a gift to you."

"A gift! What sort of gift? I've learned that there aren't any free rides in life." Ellie watches patiently as her mother and Stella size each other up. Stella reaches inside her purse and pulls an envelope out which she hands to Jenny. "Well, this may change your thinking about 'free rides'!"

Jenny opens the envelope so she and Ellie can view the contents together. It's a check for $1 million.

Jenny and Ellie look at each other in amazement. "Look, Ms. Chastain, I'm not sure what your game is, but I don't find this particularly amusing. I mean, a million dollars right out of the blue?"

"I totally understand your confusion, but I wish to assure you that this gift is totally on the up and up. You're welcome to telephone the attorney listed on the attached letterhead to confirm the check's legitimacy."

"But, I don't understand. People don't just give strangers a million dollars, at least not on the planet I live on."

"The attorney, Mr. Daniels, and I represent a wealthy individual who wishes to remain anonymous. You and Ellie have had to overcome a lot of heartache in your life, and our client wishes to be helpful to you."

Jenny and Ellie stare at each other, and then at the check again, and back at Stella. "So, you're telling us that this check is real, and we can do with it as we please."

"Yes, your benefactor hopes that much of it will be used to help fund any ongoing medical needs that Ellie may have and her formal education. The only proviso is that you not speak of this gift to anyone. Are you comfortable with that?"

Jenny's demeanor softens as Stella once again reassures them that the gift is totally real.

"I can't believe it, can you, Ellie? A million dollars!"

Ellie is nearly speechless and wheels her chair closer to Stella. "We can't thank you and your, uh, client enough, but thank you so much," and she leans forward to give Stella a warm hug.

"But, I still don't understand why we were chosen for this?" Jenny says. "I mean, there are a lot of people that are in far greater need than we are, right, Ellie?!"

Ellie shakes her head in agreement, but then laughs and says, "But, we'll gladly take it, and we promise to stay mum about this and put it to very good use."

The mood among the three of them lightens even more, and Stella says, "As far as the reason why you were selected, let's just say that you were recommended by the friend of a friend because of your hard work and good hearts, and that's all I can really say. You're welcome to write a thank-you note to Mr. Daniels acknowledging receipt of this gift, but I can assure you that neither he nor I will divulge the source of this gift."

Stella stands up, and says, "I promised not to stay long, and it's been a long day, so I'll excuse myself now."

Ellie gives Stella another hug, and Jenny embraces the two of them. "Please thank our mystery man, and rest assured that we'll do all that we can to not disappoint him or you."

"We know you won't." Then, Stella turns, blows them both a kiss, and steps contentedly out into the night air.

Chapter Eighteen

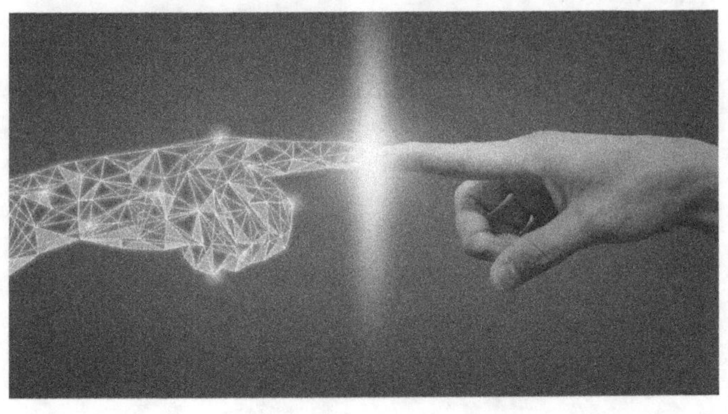

AFTER STELLA LEAVES Jenny and Ellie, I receive a call from her confirming that she's just left their house.

"All went well, I assume?"

"Yes, very well. Jenny was understandably very dubious at first, but a million dollar check with an attorney's letter attesting to its veracity has a way of reassuring the most doubting of Thomases!"

"That's great, Stella! Thanks for being a part of what we're doing, and I'll be sure to tell Marlita."

We hang up, and I stare into space thinking about the gifts we've made since winning the lottery and likely prospects for other life-enriching surprises.

~ The Birthday Gift ~

I call our son, Chris, in Chicago and say, "I have a bit of a dilemma and a possible solution that I'd like to get your advice on."

"Oh, you don't have enough dough to pay for your next meal?" he laughs as only Chris can.

"Funny!" I reply sarcastically. "No, this is a very serious dilemma involving your mom, but like I said, I may have a rather brilliant solution."

"Okay, what's the dilemma?"

"Your mom's upcoming significant birthday is July 11. She's told me repeatedly that she doesn't want any party or any gifts."

"I know. She's said the same thing to me and Elizabeth, but I agree with you, we've got to do something."

"Well, I did manage to get her to agree to our having a nice, spacious greenhouse built onto the rear of the barn. I knew that if it involved gardening, it'd be an easier sell, but I have another thought in mind that I want to privately share with you."

We chat for several minutes longer, and Chris loves my idea and offers to contact his aunts and cousins to participate.

Marlita's parents, Alan and Donna Stanley, were about as lovely and kind as any people you could ever meet. They both passed away a few years ago, but their influence and memories remain fresh. I'll never forget the first time I met them at their lovely home where Marlita, Linda, and BJ grew up. It was a beautiful ranch-style house with a terrific pond and wooded yard.

Now, I knew that Marlita and her sisters grew up in a very wholesome home where smoking, drinking, and cursing were verboten. In fact, in all of the years that I knew them, I never heard Al Stanley utter an unkind word about anybody or ever curse. Being the smart-ass that I am, I'll never forget asking Alan if he'd drop the f-bomb if I gave him a hundred dollars. As expected, he said, "Oh nooo!" I then offered him two hundred dollars, and Alan laughed and said, "You're getting closer!" That was just him, a true gentleman surrounded by us snarky relatives.

Alan owned his own engineering company, and he also served for many years as the elected Putnam County Surveyor. Donna worked in the office and kept fastidious books and records. In their free time they loved to be out in nature and would hike in the woods looking for deer and turkeys. I also probably never met a better fisherman than Al.

Through my civic contacts, I knew state and county officials involved with land management and the parks' board, and I asked Joe Daniels to approach a few of those folks about a special project. When they learned the size of the financial gift and the purpose that Joe presented to them, they were more than happy to make it possible and agreed to remain silent about it until the appointed day.

So, July 11th finally came, and it was a glorious sunny day to celebrate Marlita's birthday. "Hey, you wanna go for a drive in the country? I thought maybe we could drive down Manhattan Road and see what's happening near Vic and Lin's property."

I fibbed and said that Vic had mentioned something about a new conservation project the park board was undertaking.

"Yes, it's a lovely day, but I was thinking of just staying home and working in the garden."

"Well, there's always time for that, honey, plus I told Vic and Lin that we might swing by their place to see their new solar array and hydroponics building. Why don't we leave here about one o'clock?"

Marlita relents and agrees that the weeds in her garden can wait another day. We eat a nice, healthy lunch and then climb into Pappy for the twenty-minute drive through Greencastle, Limedale, and into the country. I take a turn onto a secluded county road, and Marlita asks me where the heck I'm going.

"Trust me," I say. In a couple of minutes we come to a mature forest and see a bunch of cars parked in a newly graveled parking area.

"What's this all about?" Marlita wonders out loud, and then she sees her sissies, BJ and Linda, and their kids, and at least another forty friends and folks from her yoga classes.

Marlita shoots me a strange look and says, "Nathan, you didn't do what I think you've done, have you?"

I feign ignorance and grin like a self-assured knucklehead.

Chris and Elizabeth approach her side of the car and open the door.

"Happy birthday, Mom!" they shout, and Marlita is surrounded by scads of well-wishers.

"Nathan! You promised me that you wouldn't go to any special effort for my birthday."

"Yeah, well, I lied!" And, I give her a hug and a peck on her cheek. "But wait, sweetheart, there's more."

We all wander over to a makeshift podium and a wooden sign covered by a white sheet. The rustling of voices finally dies down as County Commissioner Clint Berry begins speaking into a microphone. Marlita is embarrassed by the attention she's receiving and gently pokes me in the ribs. "You promised me, Nathan!" she admonishes again.

"Yeah, well, whatever! Right, Chris?"

"You'll like this, Mom!"

Clint begins, "Marlita, we're all here today because we know you wanted a huge party on your birthday," he fibs, "but Nathan and your family all thought this would be a gift that you wouldn't turn down."

Marlita looks at me for clarification, but I just shrug my ignorance, and Clint motions for a park staffer to remove the sheet over the new park sign. It reads *Alan and Donna Stanley Nature Preserve*.

Tears of joy immediately fill Marlita's eyes as she hears Clint declare this new five-hundred-acre county park is in memory of her parents. "In addition to this newly protected land, we'll also be constructing and staffing a new wildlife interpretive center that will be free and open to the public in perpetuity."

My lovely Marlita looks at me, still with tears in her eyes, embraces me, and whispers, "Thank you, darling, I never could've received a more meaningful gift."

Chris and I wink at each other like the loving coconspirators that we are, and I say to my lovely bride: "C'mon, honey, let's go greet everyone and enjoy the birthday party you *forbade* us to arrange."

Chapter Nineteen

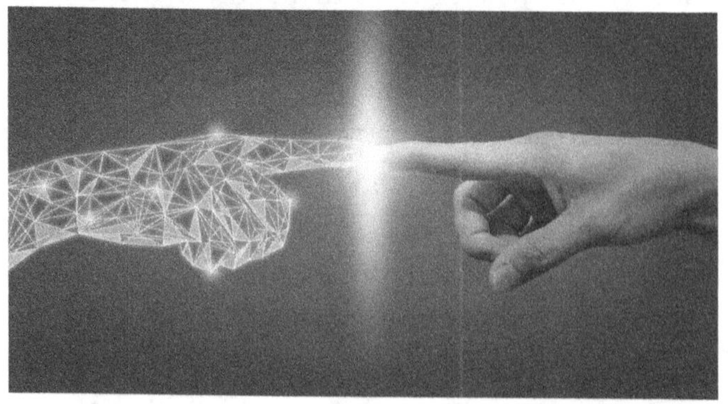

SEVERAL WEEKS PASS, and I've continued to write new chapters in *Given Names*. I love it when the words just seem to flow rather effortlessly. I remember listening to an interview with famed novelist James Patterson when he was asked if he ever gets writer's block, and he basically said, "Look, the stories either flow or they don't." I couldn't agree more.

But, there are times when it's good for me to do other creative things, too, like photographing the night sky. I've found that even when I take a brief break from writing, it's not like I've ceased being a writer. I just process my creative juices in a different way, and when I do return to my manuscript, I often find that my thoughts are fresher.

So, here I am in late July with a New Moon having already set in a pitch-black sky. Around midnight I load my camera gear and tripod into Pappy and drive to a neighbor's property that has a large, old red barn. From a previous visit I know that my best view of the barn is looking north. Ordinarily, I like to face in a southerly direction and shoot the galactic center of the Milky Way in all of its splendor, but facing north gives me an opportunity to photograph something else truly spectacular…star trails.

And the beauty of facing north is that the star trails form multiple circular patterns around Polaris, the North Star. To capture the best image, I know I need to keep my shutter open for at least two hours. This gives me ample time to think about other things, like the next chapter in my book, or worrying about coyotes dragging me off into the bushes so their young can feed on me. Okay, I really don't fret about that last part with the coyotes, but it's an intriguing scenario to consider. Regardless, it can be a little spooky out there…in the dark…alone.

Tonight, I've also brought a canvas camp chair with me and my harmonica. I enjoy improvising soft, soulful riffs on my blues harp, but only for a few minutes because the stellar sights above provide a *visual concert* that is much more captivating. At this point most of the commercial airplanes have bedded down for the night, and my camera records the slow passage of the stars above without the intrusion of flashing lights. I won't get to see the final result until I stack all of my shots in Photoshop and blend them into one single image of circular lines forming a *cosmic halo* over this majestic hay barn.

So, two hours pass, and droplets of dew are beginning to form, and I know it's time to call it a night. In the morning I'll process my thirty, four-minute exposures in Photoshop and see what the stars have to show me. I get my gear stowed in Pappy and set off into the dark heading for home. Along the way my mind wanders from the wonders of the night sky and eventually segues back to *Given Names,* and the germ of a thought comes to me.

~ Covered Bridges ~

The first time I ever saw an old covered bridge was in wintertime near Grafton, Vermont. I'd never seen one before and was frankly fascinated that structures this magical still existed. This one was memorable also because the interior had large colorful circus posters on the lengths of its walls. I imagine it's still in good repair. Even the most feeble-minded people know that something this precious needs to be protected.

And, when I moved to Putnam County twenty years ago, I learned that our county had nine covered bridges, all constructed between 1876 and 1922. I'm not sure I've visited all of them, but so far my favorites are Houck Bridge, Dunbar Bridge, Baker's Camp Bridge, and Edna Collins. I've also learned that our next-door neighbor county has thirty-one, so there's a lot of great subject matter to photograph, day and night.

The following morning I decide to contact Rick Friedman, the director of our Putnam County Convention and Visitors Bureau. Rick and I have been friends since our days serving on the

Greencastle Summer Music Festival board together. I call Rick, and he answers on the third ring.

"Hey, Nathan, what's going on? I've been thinking about calling you. I really enjoyed your last book. Great that you're giving attention to our community."

"Thanks, Rick, I appreciate that. Yeah, there are a lot of fascinating places around here, and just wait until you read the story I'm writing now. Listen, I was wondering if you're free to meet for coffee or lunch soon. I've got some questions about our covered bridges and was hoping you could bring some literature too?"

"Sure, how about having lunch at Almost Heaven day after tomorrow? Nathan, you know you can get a lot of the same information I have online, right?" "Yeah, but I'm also curious to hear more about your marketing plans for Putnam County tourism."

"You want to make a huge contribution, Nathan? We have a lot of appealing naming opportunities for different gift levels."

"You're a great salesman, Rick, I sure wish I could do something huge, but I'm just a humble writer trying to make ends meet. Besides, it's been way too long since we caught up, and I just want to see your pretty face again and hear what the CVB is up to. And yes, day after tomorrow works fine for me."

"Excellent, Nathan. I'll see you then, and sure, I've got some bridge literature I can pull together for you."

Two days later I drive Pappy into town and park on the courthouse square a couple of doors down from the entrance to Almost Heaven. Now, I've already professed my love for the Monon's diner food, but when Marlita and I want to enjoy a quiet dinner out, it's Almost Heaven where we generally choose to go. It has a lovely decor, and the food is delicious. The owner, Gail, is a highly regarded restaurateur with decades of culinary experience and scores of dedicated customers. On top of that she's a very savvy businesswoman.

When I arrive Rick is already seated in the dining room having a conversation with Gail. "Hi, Nathan, I was just congratulating Gail on being named Putnam County's Citizen of the Year by the Chamber of Commerce."

"Isn't that something?!" I add. "And very well deserved. Congratulations, Gail!"

"Oh, you two are just angling for a free lunch, aren't you?"

"No, it's all true, but if you want to give us a free lunch we wouldn't want to be rude and decline, would we, Nathan?"

"I think we can pay our way, Rick. This lady works too hard to be giving away the profits." I sit down, and Gail motions for one of her new servers named, Autumn or May or Sunshine or something to take our orders.

"So here's the literature you requested about our covered bridges. Are you thinking about showcasing them in a new book?"

"I am. In fact, I've already begun a new chapter including them, and now I need a few more details to make sure the whole vignette isn't total fiction."

"Well, I look forward to reading it when you're done. I gotta say I'm amazed at how prolific you are with your stories. What is this new book, number nine?"

"Thanks, it's actually number ten, and I just want to keep writing for as long as the spirit moves me, but I swear sometimes I feel like I'm living in two separate worlds."

We chat a bit about the CVB's upcoming marketing plans and then focus on the covered bridges.

"So, Rick, who actually owns and maintains the bridges?"

"Putnam County owns the bridges, and the commissioners are responsible for their maintenance."

"Are the bridges on the National Register of Historic Places, and do they qualify for federal money?"

"Good questions. They're not currently on the National Register, but a group of local preservationists have hired a firm to begin the application process, and the county commissioners have given their blessing to that. Keep in mind that a listing on the National Register is 'honorific' and adds no additional restrictions to the upkeep, but with the National Register listing we become eligible for some preservation dollars. Then, too, since the bridges are deemed historically significant, some restrictions are already in place for any projects involving federal money."

"Sounds complicated to me. Wouldn't we just be better off not taking any federal dollars?"

"Of course, but the feds have a lot of dough, much more than the State of Indiana and our little Putnam County. So, it's a trade-off."

"Hmm, Any idea how much the county spends every year on maintenance?"

"I don't know off the top of my head, but I'm sure the commissioners could tell you. Can't be cheap, though, especially if one's in really bad repair."

I nod my understanding. "Thanks for sharing this, Rick. There's a lot of romance around the idea of having cool covered bridges, but we obviously still need to pay for these gems."

We enjoy our lunch and chat for another thirty minutes or so, and Rick tells me he's gotta run to a meeting. After he leaves I pay for lunch and walk outside to Pappy. I sit behind the wheel thinking about our conversation, then pick up the phone and call Joe.

"Howdy, when you've got some time, I'd appreciate your looking into the details about ownership and maintenance of Putnam County's nine covered bridges. I'd like to get a feel for how much it would cost annually to cover maintenance costs without getting involved in federal dollars. I don't know the best way to proceed, but I'm thinking that maybe we should establish a separate fund for the commissioners to have access to. Depending on what you learn and what your gut tells you, perhaps we should set up a meeting with the county commissioners, the preservation people, and our Putnam County Community Foundation. I'd like to preserve these great structures without being beholding to the feds."

"Yeah, I'll be happy to do that, Nathan. During my last visit there, Stella suggested that she show me some of the bridges."

"Cool, you do know, Joe, that some folks refer to them as the kissing bridges, right?"

"Hmm, even more reason for me to do my homework and pay you guys a visit."

Chapter Twenty

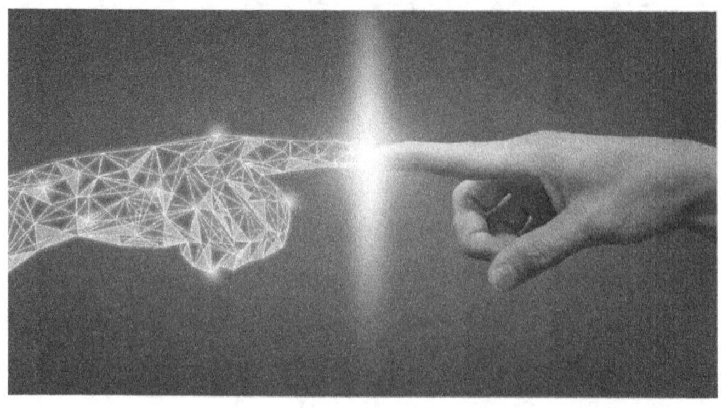

A COUPLE OF WEEKS come and go, and Joe returns to Greencastle. He's done a lot of research into the covered bridges and sets up a meeting among the concerned parties. I think he totally shocked everyone at the meeting when he announced that a client he represents has decided to contribute $3 million to a donor-advised fund at the community foundation, giving the county commissioners access to additional maintenance funds. As usual, Marlita's and my names are never mentioned, and Joe's only request of the group is to have quarterly financial statements about how any money is spent. Everyone's happy.

A few weeks prior to that, I'd also asked Joe to prepare another check for $1 million for the Putnam County Animal Shelter, and to see about delivering it to the director, Gus Miles. Hopefully, there won't be a petulant animal control officer gumming up the works this time.

After meeting with the folks about the covered bridge fund, Joe picks up Stella at the Monon, and they meet with Gus. To say that they shocked the bejesus out of him with the gift is an understatement.

"Gus, there's only one proviso that our client has for this gift," Joe informs him. "We'd appreciate it if you'd have a special bronze wall plaque made with these words and let me know when it's ready."

Gus looks at the wording for the plaque and enthusiastically agrees. Three weeks later I receive a call from Joe saying that he'd spoken with Gus who informed him that the expansion at the shelter is complete, and everything's set for our next surprise.

It's a gorgeous late summer morning in Putnam County, and I suggest to Marlita that we treat our good friend, Dutch Vanderhaar, and her lovely daughter, Lisette, to lunch and a drive in the country. She knows the little scheme I have in mind and smiles broadly as I pick up the phone to call Dutch.

"Howdy, Dutch, it's your number one male fan in Putnam County calling you."

"Jerry Rud, is this you?!" she laughs.

"Ha ha, real funny, Dutch," but in reality I can't quibble with her snarky reply because Jerry's been such a devoted friend to Dutch for many years and always made himself available to walk her little dog, Wags, before he croaked and went to pee on the great fire hydrant in the sky.

"Dutch, we were thinking this is such a beautiful day, and we haven't seen you and Lisette in a coon's age. Are you up for us taking you guys to the patio at the Fluttering Duck for lunch and a little ride in the countryside afterward?"

I hear a muffled conversation between Dutch and Lisette, and she comes back on the phone. "That would be lovely, dear boy! What time should we expect you?"

"Great! How about eleven thirty so we can beat the lunch crowd?"

"We'll be ready…and thank you!"

Marlita and I arrive at the appointed hour, and see our acquaintance Tess working in her garden. "Hi there! Great day to be working outside," Marlita affirms. "You're still taking care of everyone, aren't you?"

"Yes, but only for a few very special clients like Dutch. I don't know if you heard, but I've started my own sunflower business so I don't have as much time as I used to."

Marlita glances at me with a private smile. "Really?! That's wonderful, Tess. How many acres have you planted?"

"Oh, about five for now, but if my business takes off, I've got plenty of room to plant more. I'm pretty happy about it, and so are the birds and the bees and the little critters hiding amid the stalks."

"Well, that sounds wonderful, Tess. We're delighted for you!"

A moment later Lisette appears at the front door and holds it open for her mom. I watch as they carefully walk down the front steps and meet me at Pappy. Now, I'm not rightly clear on what Dutch's infirmity is, but she relies on a cane to steady herself.

"G'morning, ladies, and how are we on this fine day?"

"We're doing great, aren't we, Mum? We're hungry and ready for a little country scenery afterward."

"Oh, dear boy, this was a great idea, and Marlita, you're looking all chipper and everything!"

"Thanks, Dutch, what's not to be chipper about on such a glorious day, right?"

I help guide Dutch to the open rear passenger door and watch as she lifts a hip and glides into position. Okay, maybe 'glides' isn't the exact term to use, but at age ninety sumthin' our pal Dutch is doing better than a lot of people. We get her settled inside and help clip her seatbelt for her.

"All set, everybody?!" I ask, and a moment later we back out of her driveway, wave goodbye to Tess, and head off for the Fluttering Duck. When we get there I drop the three ladies off by the curb and go to park Pappy across the street. As I walk from the lot to join the ladies I see Rick Friedman from the convention and visitors' bureau at the corner.

"Hey there, Nathan, good to see you. Did you hear the wonderful news about the big gift the community foundation received to help maintain the covered bridges?"

"Yeah, I saw Red Jergens's article in the *Banner.* Great news!"

"I found it a little coincidental that you and I talked about funding for the bridges a few weeks prior to that. You didn't have anything to do with it, did you?"

"Who me? Naw, I'm just a rakishly handsome writer living in the middle of nowhere." I wink at him.

"So, do you know this Joe Daniels fella who delivered the check recently?"

"Maybe," I reply evasively. "Hey, always good to see you, Rick, but I've gotta scoot. I have three beautiful women waiting on me."

Rick sees Marlita, Dutch, and Lisette sitting outside at a patio table and waves to them.

"I'm beginning to think you're a man of mystery, Nathan Andrews."

"Who me?! And, don't forget 'rakishly handsome'!"

The ladies and I enjoy a very tasty lunch, and we each see people that we know which isn't unusual living in a small town. After lunch I retrieve Pappy and meet the ladies at the curb again. We pile ourselves back into the truck and head off into the warm afternoon sunlight.

While the ladies chatter away, I navigate Pappy past Barney's grocery store, Hadley's hardware, and Walmart. Then, I turn right on Airport Road and before long we're enjoying the countryside. I always smile to myself when I see our Putnam County Airport because it reminds me of two novels I wrote recently featuring planes that my fictional Engel family owned and hangared there. Great stories, if I do say so myself!

At this point the soybean fields are lush and green and the field corn is, well, "as high as an elephant's eye." Ten minutes later I see the entrance to the animal shelter and drive through the gate.

"Oh, are you thinking about getting a puppy or a kitty?" Lisette asks from the back seat. I look in my rearview mirror and see that Dutch is suddenly quiet with a wistful look on her face. I surmise she's thinking about her wonderful little dog, Wags, who she humanely put down recently. Our critters bring us so much joy, but at some point we have to say goodbye.

"Why don't we get out for a minute?" I suggest.

Reluctantly Dutch slides out of Pappy, and the four of us are greeted by Gus Miles.

"Hello everyone, welcome! How can we help you today?"

"Oh, we were just taking a ride in the country," Marlita says, "And, we thought we'd stop by and see what's new."

"Well, we always have a good number of dogs and cats that are available for adoption, and we've redone our lobby area and added a new, spacious outdoor run."

Marlita and I smile at each other knowingly and watch Dutch as she walks toward the lobby entrance.

"Wow, this is very nice!" she says. "A lot brighter and friendlier looking than the former shelter."

"Yeah, we were blessed recently with a substantial contribution that allowed us to upgrade our facilities and add another staff person. We still plan on making some additional upgrades, too, like a special atrium area where folks and their children can get to know their prospective pets better."

"Oh, who was the donor?" Lisette inquires.

"Don't rightly know. An attorney from Cincinnati came to see me a while back and brought a rather substantial check."

"That's wonderful," I add.

"Yeah, he said he represented a client who wanted to make certain that our shelter was the best it could be for our furry friends. He had only one condition."

"And, what was that?" Dutch asks.

Gus points to a large bronze wall plaque above the entrance to the door. "That we affectionately name this central area and the new run outside as 'The Wags Welcome Center.'

A tear comes to Dutch's eye when she sees the impressive signage, and she leans against me. "I don't suppose you and Marlita know anything about this, do you, Nathan?" she queries sweetly.

"Who us?" I say with a smile. "Well, maybe… Wags lives on!"

"Thank you, dear boy, from the bottom of my heart."

"You're very welcome, Dutch!" I whisper to her. "Let's please keep this as our little secret though, okay?"

She gently squeezes my hand, looks me in the eye, and says, "Of course, Nathan. We're pals!"

Chapter Twenty-One

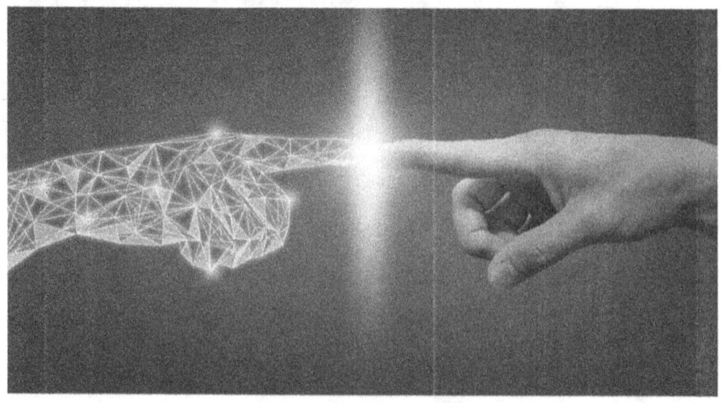

BELIEVE IT OR NOT, not all of our large monetary gifts go as smoothly as we'd like. After all, we're talking about human beings and money, right? So, even the best laid plans can sometimes go awry. Earlier today, I got a call from Stella alerting me that Matt Matlock had called her from the Putnam County Public Library with some unexpected news.

"Hi, Matt, so how are things at the library?"

"Overall, things are very good, Stella, but there is something I need to discuss with you."

"Oh, am I late returning a book, or something?" she jests.

"No, it's about our young friend, Travis Snyder. He's experiencing some family turmoil."

"I'm very sorry to hear that. What's going on?"

"Remember I shared with you that his stepdad was experiencing poor health because of his lifestyle choices?"

"Yeah, meaning that he was drinking and smoking way too much?"

"Right, well apparently his liver and kidneys failed, and he died over the weekend."

"Whew, alcohol abuse is such a sad way to die, not to mention all of the collateral damage it causes within the family. How's Travis holding up?"

"He seems to be okay. He and his stepdad were never very close, but he's much more concerned about his mother. Apparently, her husband ran through whatever little money they had drinking and gambling, and she's broke."

"That's truly tragic. I guess the good news is that Travis promised he'd open his own personal bank account and not share the details of our gift to him with his parents. Hopefully, he still has a chunk of that initial $40,000 left."

"He said he does. He told me he paid $12,000 to Indiana University for the first year's tuition, but he's really concerned about how his mom's going to make ends meet."

"Oh, dear…I swear that young fella has had enough on his mind. He's had to grow up fast."

"Travis told me that he needs to be there for his mom, so he's contacted the university about delaying his college career until things at home become more stable. He's coming home to live with her, and he's asked me for his old job back at the library. He's also very concerned about losing the money your friend gave him and letting me down. I told him not to worry about me, but I wanted to share this news with you and get your reaction regarding his future with school, etc."

"Well, it says a lot about Travis, wanting to delay his dreams to be there for his mother. I sure don't see my contact throwing the kid under the bus for something beyond his control. Let me make a call, though, just to confirm things, okay?"

"Yeah, thanks, Stella, I've told him he can come back to the library, and that I thought he should be okay going back to the university once things get sorted out, but obviously, I need to be forthright with you."

"Well, Matt, I'm glad you called, and like I said, let me make a phone call to confirm his status."

———

"So, Nathan, that's the reason for my call to you this morning. Matt's really continuing to be a good mentor and friend to Travis."

"I see. Well, the last thing I want to do is crap on this kid's dream. Please reassure Matt that Travis can take his time to help his mom through her grief, and that we're going to back him no matter what. Do you have any idea if they've got any big bills facing them?"

"No, I don't. Matt and I didn't get into specifics, but I'd be surprised if they didn't. I doubt if she and her husband owned their house free and clear, and then, of course, there's the prospect of outstanding medical bills, and who knows whatever else."

"Right. Listen, I'll give Joe a call and ask him to prepare another check. Any suggestion on how much they might need?"

"Well, first of all, thank you for being so generous, and I'll have to speak with Matt again and see if he knows about any outstanding debt they might have. I'll get back to you after I speak with him."

"Sounds good, Stella. I'm not a very religious guy, but I swear, '*There but for the grace of God go I.*'"

But, the disappointments associated with some of our gifts didn't end there. Marlita and I have always been creative and have appreciated the artistic efforts by others in our community. One thing I learned a long time ago from my father is that making a living relying on selling one's art is a very difficult road to travel. I mean, even if you sold a dozen paintings at $1,000 apiece, it still doesn't come close to making enough to support oneself, let alone a family. And, if artists use a gallery to sell their work, then the gallery is going to demand

25 to 40 percent, often forcing artists to raise their prices beyond what many people are willing to pay. And then, there are picture framing expenses and the cost of equipment and supplies. Jeez, it seems to never end. "Everybody makes it but the artist," my dad used to say, and so it seems that an artist needs to also teach in order to make a living, and hopefully have enough energy left at the end of the day to be creative.

Yeah, being an artist or owning a shop that exhibits art is definitely a tough road, but it's also something that Marlita and I still believe in. In retrospect, it was probably a weak moment when we decided to "invest" in a bright, talented, energetic young woman who wanted to open a trendy gallery in Greencastle, just off the square near the old Hathaway's building.

Using Stella as our 'agent,' we anonymously gave Mindy $75,000 to lease gallery space and open her doors. Before long the word got out about her new shop called The Muse, and lo and behold, people starting coming and buying paintings, prints, photographs, pottery, and jewelry. She wasn't making a killing selling art, but she was able to sell a few of her own paintings, too, and financially keep her head above water.

That was until some vandals busted through her back door one evening while she was working late, robbed her, and totally trashed the joint, just out of pure cussedness. It was a total mess, and Mindy was so traumatized and heartbroken by the loss and damage that she never fully recovered emotionally. The cops never found the young perpetrators, and Mindy was left with a lease she couldn't afford and inadequate insurance to cover the losses of her participating artists. A lot of people got hurt. She closed The Muse a month later, planned to declare bankruptcy, and moved to Bloomington.

Marlita and I aren't the least bit sorry we supported Mindy's dream, and the loss of the seventy-five grand isn't affecting our lifestyle, but we still feel a hefty pang of disappointment nonetheless. Since then, we've vowed to continue to anonymously help people and organizations we want to see succeed, and honestly, we make decisions based on information we have at the time, and there was no way we could've anticipated what would happen to Mindy and The Muse. Life can be cruel.

One thing that I was more than happy to under-write was an expansion of Marlita's yoga studio and the gardens surrounding the building. Talk about having a happy partner! We not only doubled her studio size but also expanded and enhanced the bathroom and storage space for her props. While we were at it, we also created a bona fide parking area so we didn't have a bunch of cars and trucks parked in our driveway during classes. Marlita has never needed to own a lot of "stuff," but what she's done with her new visual decor and an improved music system have been extremely creative. Now, even more people are coming to her already popular classes. Thank heavens for the new parking area!

It's funny when I think back to when I first won the Whopper Ball lottery and swore that I'd follow sage counsel from Joe Daniels about not spending or giving away a boatload of money for at least three months. Well, that concept worked okay for about two weeks, but when you have over $265 million, I mean, life's not a dress rehearsal, right?

Now, I've already confessed that I'm not a per-fect guy, and truth be known, I've had some episodes in my life when I didn't show as much character as I should have. I won't give you the perverse pleasure of knowing exactly how badly I misbehaved with one woman in particular, but suffice it to say, that I left a lovely lady waiting at the altar. Not one of my proudest moments! So, in an effort to assuage my guilt feelings, I prevail upon Joe to prepare and deliver a check to her for a million dollars.

"So, how'd it go when you visited with Lainy?" I ask nervously.

"It went pretty well."

"Uh huh," I reply. "Did she want to know who the money was from?"

"Of course, she did, but I didn't tell her it was from you."

"And, did she say anything else?"

"Uh, yeah. As I was leaving her house, she thanked me very much and said, 'Tell Nathan Andrews I still think he's an asshole!'"

"Oy!" I deserved it...

As for spending more money on ourselves, at our ages we really should be thinking more about getting rid of some things and downsizing. We've decided, though, to make some improvements to our house, like buying new carpet for the upstairs which I've been promising we'd do forever, plus a few other little improvements; but in the main, our home and lifestyle are very comfortable.

Another thing we originally promised ourselves was that we wouldn't buy another home somewhere, especially because we can afford to rent or lease virtually any place in the world that we want. But, as time's gone on, we're both beginning to think how nice it'd be if we had a wonderful home near Tucson fairly close to Sabino Canyon. Marlita would be in heaven, and I would have clear, dry nights to shoot the Milky Way. It's something we've begun to talk about, especially because it could be great for the kids and our friends. No rush! We'll figure it out.

Now, having said all of that, I do enjoy owning "stuff." I'm a collector at heart. When I first moved here nearly twenty years ago, I brought my antique camera collection with me, but it wasn't practical or fair for me to have over one hundred cameras staring at us from every corner of every room, so I ended up selling most of them and using some of the proceeds to build our original studio. Alas, I've always missed my beautiful wooden and brass view cameras from the nineteenth century and have recently purchased a couple of truly fine pieces that I've found online. I love 'em!

And, collecting for me was a learned 'habit.' Years ago I became good friends with a guy who was a collector par excellence. His name was L.D., and the good news for him was that he came from a very wealthy family which afforded him the opportunity to purchase virtually whatever he wanted. For L.D. that initially included an amazingly diverse collection of Americana consisting of gorgeous phonographs, furniture, clocks, and typewriters. He later morphed his collection to owning one of the finest William Faulkner collections on the planet. And, once he'd scratched those collecting itches, he built a collection of museum quality art nouveau furniture, artwork, and glass.

I, on the other hand, never had the kind of dough that allowed me to build such collections, but hanging out with L.D. introduced me to the kinds of wondrous collectibles that are out there and a sensibility about preserving such gems. As I've said my passion was/is for antique wooden cameras and rare optical toys from the 1800s. And, like I said, I sold many of them when I moved to the country with Marlita, but the collecting bug, which lay dormant for several years, still has a grip on me. Sadly, my friend L.D. was laid low by a lethal brain cancer ten years ago, but fond memories of my friend are alive whenever I look at several early phonographs and beautiful pieces of sculpture that he bequeathed to me. Beyond that, my idea of collecting these days is owning a stock portfolio which is a much more fluid asset than art and collectibles. But, I digress …

Okay, I've decided to digress a little longer… Some people who come into a lot of money immediately go out and buy a fancy car. I remember a dentist saying to me once: "You know, people judge you by the kind of car you drive." I was so surprised by the idiocy of his comment that I don't think I even replied. In retrospect, I should've asked, "What people? and Who gives a damn what they think?!"

I'm smiling to myself because my dad would've had the same exact reaction. Dad could afford a nice car if he chose to, but he drove the same 1972 Chevy Malibu back and forth to the university for twenty years. It was silver with a black vinyl roof. When the car was around eighteen years old, I was standing next to him when he opened the trunk, and there were areas that had rusted so badly that we could see through to the pavement.

I admonished him: "Dad, I think it's time for you to get a new car!" He replied, "What for?! It runs great." He drove it for another two years and sold it to the guy at the gas station for two hundred bucks. I'm sure that dentist guy wouldn't have been very impressed, but I still smile at how little dad cared for expensive vehicles. I'm perfectly happy with Pappy.

All right, now I'm finished digressing.

Chapter Twenty-Two

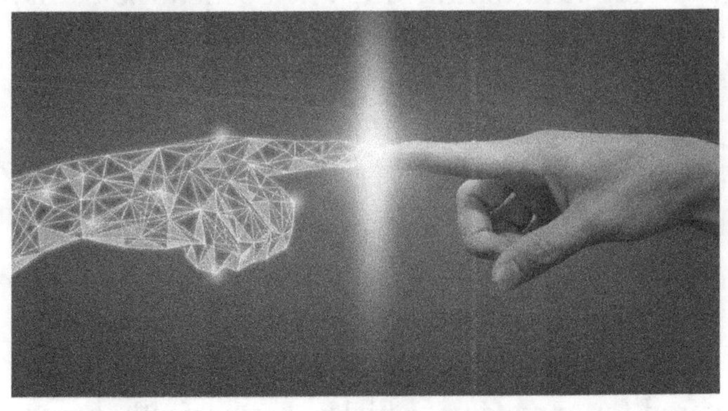

~ Putnam County Community Foundation ~
and
United Way of Central Indiana

As the summer moves on, Marlita and I start to get a feel for how much money we truly have. Even with all of the grants, gifts, and personal expenditures we've made, we've barely scratched the surface. While Marlita and I plan to continue supporting several of our charitable beneficiaries like the shelters and the library, we conclude that there are local organizations that have a much better feel than we do, including Stella, in identifying important human and cultural needs…namely, our Putnam County Community Foundation and the United Way of Central Indiana.

Back during my corporate career in Cincinnati, the United Way was a big damn deal. Top executives from major corporations like Procter & Gamble, Kroger, and others took their turns chairing annual campaigns, and none of them wanted to run a campaign that didn't exceed its financial goal. A lot of pressure was put on employees to support the annual United Way campaign, which, at the time, felt like another *tax bite* out of my paycheck. Truth is, very few people would've stepped forward on their own volition and contributed at the level our social service agencies required unless it was made very clear that we needed to do so. I understand the logic behind that and grew to feel more comfortable with my giving once I had a better understanding of the importance of our local United Way agencies like the Red Cross, United Cerebral Palsy, and the Association for the Blind. Like others, I guess I just didn't appreciate someone telling me how much to contribute. I still feel that way, but much less so since there's so much at stake.

When I moved to Putnam County, I was surprised that I didn't hear much in the way of publicity for our local United Way drives. I'm not exactly sure why, and I've hesitated saying much about that publicly because I've learned that if you shoot your mouth off, you better be prepared to step forward and take a leadership role! Having said that, I'm asking Joe to arrange a meeting with our local United Way director, Fred Cable. Joe and I'll discuss the potential size and purpose of our gift, and then we'll communicate that with Mr. Cable. For the first time, I'm thinking about Joe and me delivering the contribution together. Believe me, I understand there are risks to having people know you've got dough to give away, but there's no way they could possibly know how much I have.

So, I want to learn more from Mr. Cable about the agencies under the umbrella of our local United Way and the challenges in raising adequate funds. I want us to be helpful, but I want to give "smart money."

At the same time I want Joe to invite Miranda Terry, the director of our Putnam County Community Foundation to join us with a similar purpose. Over the years I've come to truly respect the role of community foundations which offer donors a multitude of methods to support important causes. So, I'm hoping that we can have a productive conversation about ways to make a difference, and to motivate others in our community to give more…and I have a few thoughts.

A week later, Joe is successful in arranging a meeting with Fred Cable and Miranda Terry in a private dining room at the Asbury Inn. Neither Fred nor Miranda have any concrete idea about the exact nature of the meeting, but Joe has lured them with the promise of a major surprise. When I arrive at the dining room I see Joe and the two directors already seated in anxious expectation.

"Oh, hi Nathan, I didn't know you'd be joining us too," says Miranda. Fred looks surprised at seeing me, probably wondering why the presence of a novelist is necessary.

"Hi everyone, sorry I'm a little late. Traffic near Shadowlawn and Jackson Streets was bollixed up by road repair." A server takes our lunch orders, and we make idle chitchat until a final guest enters the dining room.

"Sorry to be so late," Red Jergens says. "Thank goodness our roads are finally being repaved, but it's making a mess of our traffic." Red's the editor of the *Banner* newspaper and a good friend who's always written supportive articles about my novels. He sits down between me and Joe and looks on with pen in hand in journalistic anticipation.

I nod at Joe and he begins, "Nathan and I want to thank you all for joining us today for what we hope will be a landmark day in Putnam County. That's the reason we've invited Red to join us as well. Both the United Way and the Putnam County Community Foundation play vital roles in our community, and we've asked you here today to hopefully help make your jobs a little easier. I'm an attorney with the law firm Hoffman Fabian and True in Cincinnati, and I represent Nathan and Marlita Andrews who have a deep, personal interest in the success of Putnam County and its residents."

There's a brief silence, and Joe looks to me to continue. "Thanks, Joe, since I know you're all very busy people, I'll come right to the point. Marlita and I have recently come into a bit of money, and we wish to share it with deserving and qualified agencies through grants from your organizations."

Fred and Miranda sit up in their chairs. "That's lovely, Nathan, how much are you and Marlita thinking of contributing?"

Without blinking an eye I reply, "$10 million each." You could hear a pin drop in the room.

Red says, "Did I hear you correctly, Nathan, you did say ten million each, right?"

"I did. Now, having said that, I don't want this to be 'dumb money' that just gets donated and spent as usual. My desire is that half will be used as the principal of an endowment fund that will spin off income each year, either for grants or reinvestment, and the other five million may be used over time as your grants committees deem appropriate. I also want you both to work with your boards of directors to develop solid business plans to motivate others to support your agencies even more; principally through a program of matching gifts...and a concerted public relations campaign to showcase needs that your organizations have identified and ways that people can be helpful. I know you already do that to a large extent, but I want you to do even more so that our area becomes known as a community of givers."

Fred and Miranda look at me as if I'd consumed a psychedelic mushroom. "Are you serious, Nathan? You and Marlita have that kind of money to give?"

Both Joe and I nod our heads in affirmation. "We do."

The mood in the room suddenly goes from suspicion to elation when Joe pulls out checks in the name of each institution. "These checks are mock-ups, and if you agree to the expectations that Nathan's expressed, I'll be happy to work with our money manager and yours in transferring the real assets by the end of the week. Are we in agreement?"

"There's one final point I would like to add though." The directors look at me for the other shoe to drop, but I say, " We don't want your organizations to operate totally independently. It's our hope that there will be a concerted effort by each of you and your boards to work together in maximizing the charitable dollars you have to distribute. I know this can be a challenge, but I'd like your agreement that you'll make your very best efforts to work in harmony."

Fred and Miranda look at each other and then at me and Joe. They nod their heads and say, "Of course, Nathan, we'll be happy to do that…and thank you so much! This is incredible!"

"Red, my attorney, Joe Daniels, has repeatedly advised us not to go public with our newfound wealth, mainly for fear of how people will treat us and perhaps even abuse our privacy. You're a very clever editor, and I hope that when you publish this story, you'll try to make it clear that Marlita and I have given all of our assets away so it's pointless for folks to approach us."

"Yeah, I can definitely do that, Nathan, but don't be surprised if some folks just don't get the message. People will forever view you guys differently now."

"I know you're probably right, Red, but sometimes it's important to come out of the shadows and make a statement, and Marlita and I think it's worth the risk. So, everyone, if you're comfortable with everything we've said, let's move forward, okay?"

"Hell yes!" Fred blurts out. "I definitely second that, Nathan," Miranda chimes in. "What can we do to recognize you and Marlita? I mean, these are among the largest gifts anyone has ever made in Putnam County."

"You know, I've never been accused of having a small ego, and I like recognition as much as the next guy, but Marlita and I prefer to let the light shine on the good works that you and the agencies do. Right, Joe?"

I see a brotherly look of pride on Joe's face. "All ships rise on the same tide, my friend!"

Red Jergens looks at me with a proud smile as well. "Yeah, Nathan, I think I can write something that will help lift all our ships and keep you and Marlita away from the shoals."

At the conclusion of our lunch, we dismiss merely shaking hands and offer friendly hugs all around. Joe and I walk out of the dining room knowing we've just done something very special, believing that we've sparked opportunities for hope and prosperity for our neighbors.

"So much for anonymity, huh, Nathan?!"

As we leave the inn, I call Marlita and suggest that she meet us at the Monon to celebrate with Stella.

"Everything went very well, darlin.' Red's preparing a special article for tomorrow's *Banner*, and this may be the last time we can go out in public without receiving a lot of attention. So, let's go enjoy ourselves."

When Joe and I arrive at the Monon we hold the door open for the elderly couple we've encountered before.

"Look, dear! It's that nice author we've seen here before."

"Rice author?! What rice? I had the potatoes. Remember? Maude, I swear your memory is just not what it used to be."

"Come along, Rufus," she chirps lovingly. "No, no, sweetheart. This is our car."

She smiles at Joe and me and says, "Don't get old. It's not for sissies."

"Sissies?!" her husband declares. "I knew it the first time I saw them. Next thing ya know, they'll be spouting those funny pronouns!" She rolls her eyes, and Joe whispers to her: "Good luck!"

Stella greets us as we enter and gives Joe and me warm hugs. I notice that she seems to linger a little longer with Joe's hug and can't help but tease him a little after she trots off to get us some drinks and water.

"Joe's got a girlfriend!" I lob at him adolescently. "You're such a stud!"

In return, he simply replies, "Button it, moneybags!"

Marlita walks through the door and sees us seated at a booth. "So, what were the looks on Fred and Miranda's faces when you told them about our grants?"

"About what you'd expect. Astonished, astounded, and thunderstruck. You know, they're probably still trying to figure out where we came up with the dough, or if it's Monopoly money."

"What?! They weren't flummoxed and gobsmacked?!"

"Oh please! No one uses words like that," I toss back sarcastically.

Stella rejoins us, and we tell her about the meeting with the directors from the United Way and the Community Foundation.

"$20 million!" she blurts out, and a few diner patrons look our way. "$20 million!" she repeats in a whisper.

"Yeah, but that's combined. Ten mill each!" Joe replies. "Go big or go home, right, Nathan?!"

"So, how much do you think we've given away so far, Nathan?" Marlita asks.

"Probably about $40 million to family and various folks and good causes in the community," I reckon.

I look at Joe, and he nods his head in agreement. "Plus or minus, but keep in mind, Marlita, that if you've got over $260 million to begin with, and you give away $40 million, you've still got over $220 million left!"

"Point taken!" she laughs.

"So, Nathan, have you purchased anything really special for yourself?" Stella asks.

I shoot a smart-ass grin at Marlita."Well, we're getting new carpet for the upstairs."

Marlita rolls her eyes. "Yeah, I'll believe it when I see it."

"Soon, very soon, I promise! In fact to show you what a prince I am, just go out and get whatever you want. I've been expecting you to do that for the last six months anyway."

"Nathan, dear! Sometimes you're just insufferable!"

To show you how *insufferable* I can be sometimes, I take her sarcastic remark as a compliment.

"No, I mean something really special just for you," Stella tries again.

"A couple of great antique cameras I've sneaked into the house when 'Princess Moonbeam' wasn't looking, but otherwise, nothing of any significance. Maybe at some point I will, but I've got virtually everything I need right now."

I don't see Joe, Marlita, and Stella shoot quick glances at each other, and we change the subject to menu selections.

"Well, I can't make any dough sitting here on my derriere!" Stella declares. "I've got a diner to run!" She scoots off to other customers.

"And, it's a nice derriere, too, isn't it, Joe?!"

Joe smiles and winks at me. "Cool it, Nathan, I'm not saying anything without the benefit of legal counsel."

Chapter Twenty-Three

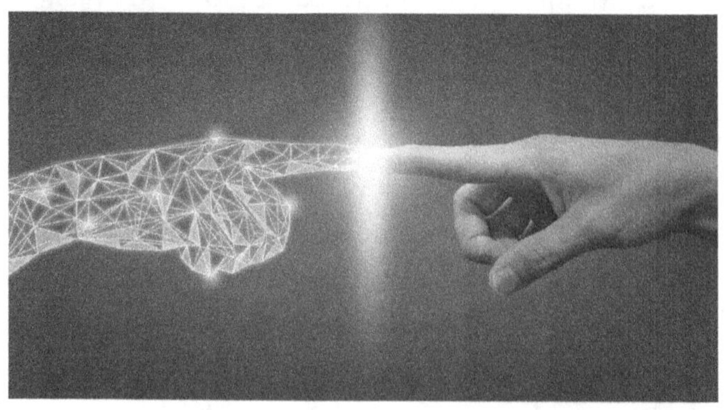

T HE NEXT MORNING Joe has a quick breakfast with Marlita and me and says he needs to get back to his office. He packs his belongings, gives us hugs, and walks to the back door. "I'll take care of those transfers to the United Way and the Putnam County Community Foundation once I've gotten their account information. I'll let you know when it's all done, Nathan."

After he leaves, my lovely wife tells me she's going to the Amish produce auction with her good pal, Cathy, over by Rockville. I always worry when she goes there because I remember the time she went, uh, *unsupervised* and came home with sixty cantaloupes. Sixty!

As Joe, Stella, Marlita, and I suspected, it doesn't take long for the news of our financial commitments to reach the public. Red Jergens's article in the morning paper heaped great praise on what the additional funds would mean to our neighbors and local organizations, and although he clearly articulated that Marlita and I had given away all of our newfound wealth, we know some people will show up on our doorstep looking for handouts nonetheless. I can't say that I blame them since a recent article in the *Banner* shared that one-third of the people in our community struggle financially. It'll be very hard to turn some people away, but over time, hopefully most folks will get the message, and the number of visitors should decline.

I walk upstairs to my office and find Bella already sitting on my desk. "How about you write the next chapter in *Given Names*, Bella? I'm not really feeling the muse this morning."

She swats at a housefly and bounds away after it, leaving me pondering the next chapter and the scope of gifts Marlita and I have given away in just a few months. I feel a real sense of satisfaction in the decisions we've made so far but think it's probably time to slow down our giving for a while. I'd sure hate to burn through $260 million in just a few months, as if that's even possible.

After puttering around in my office, though, I decide there's another great local cause that I haven't given special attention to yet. I get cleaned up and decide to drive back into town.

~ Putnam County Museum ~

Okay, I must admit up front that when I came to live here twenty years ago, I wasn't impressed by what we called our county museum. I mean, it was what it was…a collection of history, art, and artifacts representing the lives and enterprises of Putnam County residents, but in a modest way. Over time, however, I've really come to admire the growth the museum has experienced thanks to very good management, dedicated volunteers, and a supportive board.

Marlita and I have always been members, but we've never stepped forward to contribute in a larger way, including our annual membership gifts. I exit Pappy, approach the museum building, and see the rusty old farm implements sitting proudly on the front walkway. To me, they look princely in their well-earned retirement.

I enter and inhale the full-bodied aroma that the museum exudes. To me as a collector, it's almost like a pheromone. I step up to the front desk and see my dear friend Anita Mack with a big smile on her face greeting me as I arrive.

"Well, if it's not my favorite author! Nathan, it's been too long. I trust you and the lovely Marlita are getting along famously? And, I hope you're busy working on a new novel."

"Anita, you've always been my number one fan. Marlita and I are doing very well, thank you. She keeps really busy around our place, and I try to look busy whenever she's around. And, yes, I'm working on a new novel. The title is *Given Names*, and it's a totally new story with all new characters.

It's semiautobiographical and semifiction. and that's all I'm gonna tell you for now…"

"But, I'm your number one fan, Nathan," she replies and fakes woeful disappointment.

"Okay, but this is all I'm gonna tell you: It's about this roguishly handsome writer living in Putnam County, and he wins the lottery, like beaucoup bucks!"

"And!" she prompts me.

"And, that's all I'm gonna tell ya. You'll have to read the book when it's done."

"Ooh, you're a rascal, Nathan Andrews!"

"Okay, I'm gonna go look around for a bit and then see if Alisha has a few minutes for me."

"I'll go let her know you're here while you mosey around."

The first thing I see as I enter the broad hallway leading to the galleries is my large old portrait camera resting on its stout iron-and-wooden studio stand. It was too big for our home, and the museum was the perfect place for it, so here it is. I still love that old camera.

I walk down the hallway and see the terrific wildlife photographs by our friend Lynne on exhibit in the long hall. Several are very special images, and I take a few minutes to observe their details. She's got a great eye…and patience. I remember seeing her by happenstance on a very rainy, gloomy day waiting to take pictures of killdeer. I thought the lady was loony tunes hanging out on such a crappy day until I remembered that I often go out all night to take pictures, getting eaten by bugs and possibly getting carried off by coyotes! Okay, the coyote thing is an exaggeration, but the damn bugs aren't!

I move on and see our friend Lane's important pottery exhibit and smile when I notice the name Rookwood on display. As a former Cincinnatian, the name Rookwood was a famous name that I learned early in life. For decades their designers and potters created world-class ceramics that are highly sought after by collectors today. Over time, Rookwood Pottery ceased operations, and the old, large kilns and factory were converted into charming dining areas. When I lived in Cincinnati, I had the pleasure of meeting friends there on many occasions. Lane's put together a very fine collection.

From there, I see one fascinating thing after another: paintings, brass cash registers, Peeler pottery, farm tools...on and on. It's like eye-candy for me. I move into the gallery currently featuring the students' art show. I take a seat on a bench in the middle of the room and rotate very slowly as I try to take in the various paintings, drawings, collages, and mixed-media art created by our local school children. There are a couple of unspectacular pieces that I privately roll my eyes at, but several of these kids have some real talent. It's fun to see the colors and shapes of things they come up with.

"Nathan!" I hear my name called. It's Alisha Gray, the museum's director.

"In here, with the kids' art."

"There you are. I was hoping to catch you before you took off."

"So, how's the museum biz doing these days?"

"Bizzy, as usual, between changing exhibitions and planning our takeover of the entire building... finally! We sure need the additional exhibit and storage space."

"Yeah, I get it. Museums are kinda like icebergs, with probably 90 percent of the entire collection hidden from view."

"So, what brings you in today, Nathan?"

"Well, actually a couple of things. First, I just enjoy seeing what's new and exciting, and I'm impressed by several pieces in the students' show. But, I had a thought about a personal exhibition that I wanted to get your reaction to."

"Oh, what're you thinking?"

"Well, you know I enjoy photographing the night sky. I've been thinking about putting together an immersive exhibition similar to the Van Gogh exhibit that the Indianapolis Art Museum held last year."

"Wasn't that something being totally surrounded, walls, ceiling, and floor with Van Gogh's incredible work?"

"Very unique. So, I was thinking wouldn't it be fun if we held a similar exhibition of my Milky Way photos over different places in Putnam County? I can envision people walking into the gallery and being surrounded by scenes of thousands of stars, planets, and the moon. Perhaps, we could even do it as a nice fundraiser for the museum."

"Wow, I love that idea, Nathan! Your photography is amazing, and I'm always looking for unique fundraising ideas. I doubt if we have the projection capabilities like the Van Gogh exhibit, though."

"I understand, but I'd be willing to help fund the purchase of new equipment, if necessary, and perhaps a printed catalog of the exhibition."

"Wow, that's exciting! After you leave, I'll check the museum's calendar for potential dates and speak with a couple of our volunteer board members. Can I get back to you?"

"Sure, if it turns out to be something you'd like to do, just say the word. I already have some great, large photo files that should work well for large projections. Obtaining the right equipment for a totally immersive experience may be a challenge, but I think we can do it."

"So, you mentioned you had a couple of things to discuss. What else is on your creative mind?"

"Well, last month at the museum's annual meeting, you announced that plans were being made for taking over the entire building, but that a lot of money would be needed to make that happen. You said something about a capital campaign but didn't give any specifics in terms of the dollar goal and campaign leadership."

"True! It's something we definitely need to do, and our board is still wrestling with how much we'll need, both for physical improvements to our space and more endowment money to help spin off additional support for our overall operations and building maintenance going forward."

"Any idea how much you'll be needing?"

"Well, I have an idea of what I'd like for us to have but getting people to step up and contribute will likely be a real challenge."

"So, how much?" I ask again.

"Probably, about $4 million which is a boatload of money for a community like ours."

"Yes, it is! Any ideas about who you want to chair the fundraising effort and make leadership gifts?"

"Yes, but getting that person to agree to chair it could be hard. We'll see. Any thoughts on your end?"

"You may not know that prior to my moving to Putnam County twenty years ago, my career in Cincinnati was charitable fundraising, and I directed a couple of very large capital and endowment campaigns for Children's Hospital and the Cincinnati Zoo."

Alisha's ears perk up. "I didn't know that. Any interest in taking a leadership fundraising role again?"

"Not chairing a large drive, per se. After raising charitable funds for many years, I'm frankly weary of working on committees, but Marlita and I may be helpful in another leadership capacity."

"Oh? Like?"

"You say you think you'll need about $4 million, right? Plus or minus."

"Yeah, probably more plus than minus."

"What if we were to pledge $2 million but in the form of a challenge grant?"

"You mean like matching each dollar contributed?"

"Yes, but I don't want to take the pressure off of you and our community to support the effort. What if we gave the $2 million, but only after the museum raises the first $2 million?"

"I love the idea, Nathan, but even raising the first $2 million from our community could be a real challenge…and are you really serious about contributing that kind of money?"

"It would be a challenge, but yes, I'm very serious about giving that kind of dough. I'm a collector at heart, and I think the museum has a lot to offer folks of all ages. For now, I prefer that you keep this conversation within a very small orbit of museum leadership, but let me know what you guys think about my suggestion, okay?"

"I definitely will! Thank you so much, Nathan! And, I'll get back to you about a possible immersive photography exhibition, as well."

Alisha and I chat for a few minutes longer, and I stand to leave.

"You're doing a great job, Alisha, and I want you to feel like you've got the support you need. Just keep doing what you're doing. I've always found that money follows ideas."

Chapter Twenty-Four

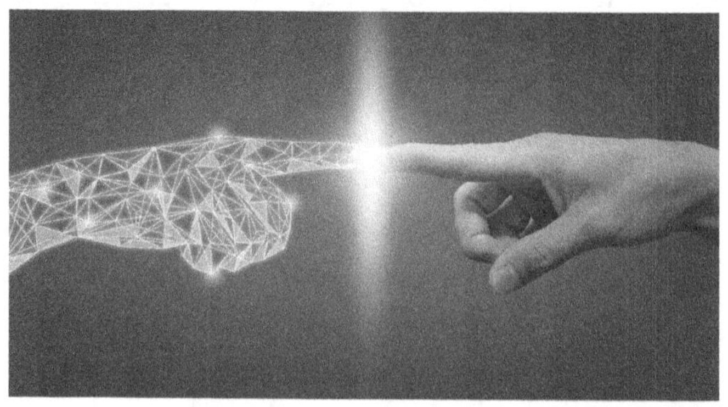

A S WE ENTER AUTUMN with its first hints of much cooler weather, I continue to focus on outdoor projects on our property. For me that means working in the flower beds around the house, loading up on firewood, keeping the garage and workshop organized, and other barnyard stuff. Marlita would be the first one to acknowledge that I'm not the handiest dude when it comes to outdoor work, except for my gardens. In fact, when I first moved here and she saw how limited my skills were at fixin'

shit, she called me, and I quote, *"A damn city pussy!"* Ouch! I might have preferred that she selected a different choice of words, but the gist of what she said runs true. No need for great intellectuals like me in the country, I reckon.

So, instead, I do what any self-respecting city feller would do, I pay others to do the work: Mowing, carpentry, painting, roofing, yup, I prefer to write checks and help keep folks in our community gainfully employed. The hard part's been finding people that are really good at their craft and show up when they say they will. I feel like we finally have a crew of good, reliable workers that we can call upon, but we sure kissed enough frogs to finally find our princes.

Thankfully, the summer and autumn months offer me a source of enjoyment that I only came to fully appreciate once I moved to the country, namely, the night sky. I mean, a dark starlit night is mesmerizing no matter the season. What's not to love about Orion, Canis Major, and Auriga in winter?! But, these days it's comfortable enough at night that I can face south and photograph the galactic center of the Milky Way for hours. Even as a writer I feel helpless in finding adequate words to describe the vast wonder, but over time I've mastered the settings on my camera to take memorable images of what I see. It never ceases to astonish!

Right now I'm sitting at my desk, and Bella is keeping me company as I write another chapter in *Given Names.* I'm excited about the way the story's unfolding, but I still have a way to go. I'm not exactly sure how I want to conclude this novel, but I reckon I'll figure it out soon enough.

I hear a ringtone from my computer and see that I've just received an email from the astronomy department at Asbury College announcing a public viewing of the night sky at the McKim Observatory tonight. Whenever possible I always like to go because the professors are friendly and informative, but mainly because the observatory's 9.53" Clark telescope is both a delight to behold and a wonder to look through. The observatory and wooden-clad telescope were built in 1884 for $10,000 which included construction of the building and a complete astronomical outfit. To an old collector like me, the polished wood surrounding the scope's main tube makes it look like a piece of antiquated technology out of a Jules Verne novel. The gleaming brass fittings and polished glass optics offer the Clark telescope additional regal bearing.

I believe I may have mentioned this, but when I arrived here in Putnam County almost twenty years ago, I came with a collection of over one hundred very early wooden-and-brass view cameras and pre-cinema optical devices like magic lanterns and such. Several of my cameras dated back to the 1850s, and many others predated the twentieth century. It was a unique collection. But, when I moved to the country, we didn't have adequate space to display them, and I didn't like the thought of just packing them away, so I made the decision to sell the majority of my cameras. I made a good profit, and we used the proceeds to build our studio onto our old dairy barn which is home to Marlita's yoga practice. But, my love of antique cameras and optical devices is like having an old friend that I want to keep forever. In the last couple of months I've seen a few really nice wooden cameras listed for sale on the internet. The ones I'd been eyeing were prime examples that dated to the mid-1800s. Beautiful, original view cameras made by early camera makers and opticians in America, England, and France…so I bought them and have them on display in my office.

So, now that I have an opportunity to go and pay homage to this magnificent nineteenth century wooden telescope and see what wonders it'll reveal, I quickly check the weather app on my phone and see that the forecast calls for mostly clear skies. There's no way I'm not going for this. The email said we'd be looking at the rings of Saturn and a few of its many moons. I'm psyched and send an email back saying I'll be there.

Marlita and I enjoy a tasty dinner she's prepared for us, and then play our usual after-dinner cribbage game. Now, I would be remiss if I didn't mention that Marlita and I take our cribbage games VERY seriously. We've played at least three times a day, virtually every day for eighteen years. My biggest regret is ever teaching her because she kicks my rear end regularly, like for stretches of days where I wonder if I'll ever win again…and then the tides turn, and I get to whomp her for several days before the tides turn again. You get the picture. But, we love our cribbage games, and it's a great way to, uh, release stress! Please don't ask if we cheat or cuss.

We finish our close game which she won, and I tell her I'm off to the observatory.

———

When I arrive I see a small line of people of different ages entering the McKim Observatory. It's great seeing parents with their children and to hear the excitement in the kids' voices about getting to see the rings of Saturn. I patiently wait in line and chat up a few people that I recognize from previous stargazing events. Some fifteen minutes later my turn is three people away, and I take a few minutes to talk with Professor Morrie Kurtz about the scope and the astronomy department's plans for the future.

It's a pretty revealing conversation in just a brief period of time. Morrie shares that Asbury College is preparing to embark on yet another major fundraising campaign which he's excited about since the college's trustees are talking about making the sciences, including astronomy, a major focus. Morrie shares that he understands that the trustees would like to make better use of the college's properties, and that an additional observatory might be built in a secluded area of the nature park. Then, it's my turn to semirecline under the eye piece of the Clark telescope, and I feel as excited as those kids I saw earlier. "Whew! What a view! I can't believe I just saw the rings of Saturn." Like I said before, "It astonishes!"

I reluctantly surrender the telescope to a young mother and her daughter, exit the observatory, and amble back toward Pappy. I gaze up at the sky and can only see a fraction of the stars I saw a few moments ago. I glance over my shoulder to look at the lovely white observatory with its gray steel dome. Man, now that's what I call a grand antique optical device! One that reveals a universe of dreams. I tuck that thought away for now.

I drive back home and tell Marlita how much fun I had tonight. "You know, I'm wondering what it would cost to construct a really fine observatory on our property, something with even greater magnification than the McKim's Clark scope. It could be pretty cool."

"Well, the good news is that you can afford to do whatever you want, but I thought we talked about the pros and cons of doing that on our property already. Didn't you come to the conclusion that we don't get that many great nights for viewing because of cloud cover and other atmospheric crud?"

"Yeah, we did."

"And, didn't you say it could be a real pain in the patootie to lug heavy equipment around and hook it up?"

"Yeah, I did."

"So?! And, don't you think it might be better to contribute to the college instead of building your own observatory and feeling compelled to use it all the time?"

"Uh, yeah, probably."

"And, don't you get enough satisfaction by simply taking your camera and tripod out instead of a bunch of heavy, awkward equipment…and wouldn't it be better for students to have regular access to another big scope on campus?"

"Okay, so building one here may not be such a good idea, after all, but a big scope would be sooo cool!"

"Well, Nathan, why don't you think about it some more? I'm sure you'll come to a wise conclusion."

And, I did think about it some more and did see the logic in her reasoning, but it would still be awesome to have one. Maybe someday.

That night I lay in bed thinking about the stars, the immensity of our universe, and how small we human beings really are in the vast scheme of things. We're on this planet for such a brief span of time, and then we're gone…all the more reason to make the best of our lives and the lives of others while we have a chance.

Chapter Twenty-Five

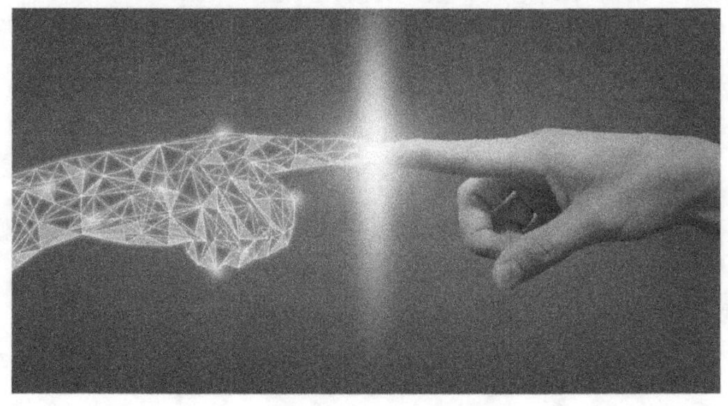

~ One Year Later ~

So, NEARLY A YEAR has come and gone since I won the Whopper Ball lottery, during which time I've had ample opportunities to consider how I've spent my previous life and consider how I want to live going forward. When you still have over $220 million, money becomes an almost abstract concept, nearly meaningless unless I do something meaningful with it. I haven't mentioned this before, but I'm coming up on my seventy-fourth birthday in a few weeks which is a rather sobering thought, and my sweet Marlita turned the big seven-o recently, too. Time is moving on for both of us, that's for sure!

When I reflect on everything that's occurred, I don't think that much about the stunning wealth that's come my way, but it's the people whose lives I've touched that's changed me the most as a person. Yeah, I'm pretty much the same frisky, spirited dude I've always been…creative, generous, and a little too full-of-myself at times, but I believe I've added a little more humility to my persona because of the major commitments I've made on behalf of others. I feel very good about that.

None of my benefaction would've been nearly as enjoyable and successful if it weren't for the wonderful roles that Joe Daniels and Stella Chastain have performed for us. I'd say both of them take their responsibilities very seriously and hopefully giggle, chortle, and guffaw at how much fun they're having. They don't know it yet, but I'm going to boost their year-end bonuses. What's another mill here or there, right? I'd be curious to know how they feel that their lives have changed as a result of their participation. And, who knows what's in store for us yet.

Once again I'm seated at my desk thinking of various ways to finish writing *Given Names*. I feel very good about the story I've composed so far and hope to have the ending meet my expectations. Bella lies peacefully on the floor next to me, and through the floor register I can hear Marlita on the phone downstairs with her sisters ostensibly planning another vacation somewhere. As long as they can hike, drink wine, and play games at the end of the day, I don't think they really much care where they go. I love that they enjoy spending time together.

I look around at several prized items in my office that I've collected over the years, looking for possible inspiration for my next novel. I find it curious that inanimate objects like my 1850s wet plate era camera can *animate* my imagination so much. Perhaps, there's a story there, maybe about all the people who've owned this 170-year-old wooden-and-brass beauty and all the people who've sat for portraits. Something to ponder.

I look around at several of my father's paintings and think about the man both as my father and as an admired painter and college professor. I'm very pleased that he lived well into his late eighties so I had a chance to get to know him as an adult. His life, itself, is worthy subject matter for a novel, but in some ways I feel like his life was filled with great accolade and that I should focus elsewhere.

I hear Marlita get off the phone with her sissies and a few minutes later see her bright, smiling face appear in my office doorway.

"Hey, it's a little after four o'clock. Do you want to take some time for a coffee break and a game of cribbage before we head out this evening?"

"Sure," I reply, "but I didn't know we were going out tonight."

"Didn't I talk with you about going to a reception at the nature park?"

"Uh, I don't think so, but that sounds like something fun. What's the occasion?"

"Asbury College is announcing a new nature program, and we've been invited to hear the president speak. I thought we could stop by and then maybe go to Almost Heaven for dinner. How's that sound?"

"Sounds good! Can I go dressed as I am in jeans and a hoodie or should I clean up my act a little more?"

"Darlin', you've been working outside today and then lounging around in the same clothes in your office, so yeah, I think you can probably make a better public appearance."

"Should we invite anyone to join us?'

"Well, it'd be very late notice, and I thought we might just enjoy a nice evening at the nature park and then a quiet dinner. Let's leave here in about an hour, though, okay?"

I save my manuscript on my computer and then shut it down.

An hour later I've shaved, showered, brushed my teeth, flossed, applied some deodorant, and combed my hair. Choosing an ensemble to wear is very easy…nice buttoned-down shirt, khaki slacks, blue blazer, my twenty-year-old Cole Haan loafers, and I'm looking *sharp as a meatball* as my dad used to tease me.

"Wow! You're smokin' hot, Princess Moonbeam!" I say to Marlita. "You look pretty gussied up for a reception at the nature park."

"What?! This old rag. I've owned it forever."

I shrug, and we walk out the door and climb into Pappy.

"Look!" I point out to Marlita in the western sky. "It's Venus looking sharp as a meatball!"

She rolls her eyes. "Drive, Nathan!"

"Yes, dear!"

When we arrive at the nature park we see that the lot is full of cars.

"I thought you said this was going to be a little reception. I bet there's a hundred cars here."

"Well, honey, apparently the college's idea of a little reception and yours might be different. Now, step lively! We don't want to be late for the president's opening remarks."

As we walk along a paved trail to an elevated area within the park, I see a gleaming new building for the first time with a domed metal roof looking like a larger twin to the McKim Observatory in town.

"Wow! Look at that! I had no idea that Asbury College had moved forward with a new astronomy facility. I'm surprised nobody told us."

She takes my hand and leads me through a throng of people, many of whom we recognize. "Wow, this looks like a big damn deal! C'mon let's sit in the back so we can leave if the presentation gets boring."

"Uh, no can do buckaroo!" I hear a familiar voice say. I turn and see Joe and Stella standing next to us with great, Cheshire-cat-like grins on their faces.

"Whoa, I had no idea you guys would be here tonight. Marlita, did you know? Joe, is this something that we're funding that I didn't know about?"

"Sorta," comes his evasive reply. "C'mon, we've saved seats for us in the front row."

I look at Marlita and whisper, "So much for sneaking out if the program's a dud!"

Then, I begin to see the faces of people that I recognize, and some I haven't seen for a while.

"Look, honey, it's Matt Matlock from the library, and he's brought young Travis Snyder with him. I need to follow up with them to see if Travis's been able to return to classes at IU.

"And, over there it's Rick Friedman from the Convention and Visitors' Bureau. Remember, Rick and I worked together with our county commissioners to keep our covered bridges in very good repair? I'm still really thrilled that we did that."

"I do remember, Nathan, and look, isn't that Miranda Terry from the Community Foundation seated with Fred Cable from United Way?" The two agency directors see Marlita and me and come to say hello.

"Great night to be out under the stars, eh Nathan?!" Miranda offers. "It's great you came to celebrate the opening of this terrific facility."

"Yeah, I must admit that I'm a little embarrassed that I don't know much about it."

"Not a problem, Nathan, I understand that President Blanco is going to make a surprise announcement tonight." We talk briefly about their promotional efforts, and then we get drawn into exchanges with other people.

I feel a light tap on my shoulder and turn to see Alisha Gray and Anita Mack from our county museum. "Well, my goodness, who's keeping an eye on the museum collection while you guys are here?" I ask playfully.

"Well, you do know that we have lives outside of the museum, don't you, Nathan?"

"Hmm, I never thought about it," I tease. "I figured you ate, drank, and slept with all the *fun toys* you've got."

"I'm eager to read your new novel, Nathan, where are you with it?"

"Close, Anita! Very close to having my first draft done. Still, not exactly sure how I'm going to finish *Given Names*, but I think it's getting pretty near."

Then, I feel another tap and see the friendly face of Reverend Langston Bryant. "My goodness, someone call security!" I laugh. "If the clergy's here, then someone must be up to no good, and this gentle man is looking to save 'em." We give each other a warm hug, and my favorite cleric says, "Let's have coffee soon, Nathan, I want to share all of the good work your support has allowed."

"Will do, Langston, always great to see you, my friend!"

From a distance I spy my lovely pal Dutch Vanderhaar with her equally lovely daughter, Lisette.

They're having a conversation with the animal shelter's Gus Miles. I'm so happy we were able to create the Wags Welcome Center at the Humane Society. Dutch catches my eye and gives me a quick wink.

"Gee, Marlita, this is starting to feel like old home week."

"We've got a lot of nice friends in this community, Nathan."

A moment later a woman approaches us who's name I've forgotten. Thankfully, she reintroduces herself before I completely embarrass myself.

"Hi, Nathan, I don't know if you remember me. I'm Rebecca Lind from the homeless shelter."

"Of course, I do, Rebecca," I fib. "Good to see you. Were you ever able to get some housing for that young Cade Willet fella who was struggling with alcohol…and life in general, I guess."

"We were. He stayed with us briefly and then moved on. About a month ago I heard from another resident who knew him that Cade had passed away. Organ failure due to his drinking."

"That's heartbreaking news, Rebecca. I really appreciate you and your staff trying to help him. That's so sad to hear, though."

"We all try to do the best we can. Fortunately, folks in our community are supportive of our mission, but we don't always succeed."

I look at Rebecca firmly in the eye and say, "I don't want you to be shy about approaching me if you need something for the shelter. If you need some help, just say so, okay?" Marlita gives my hand a sweet squeeze.

"Thank you, Nathan, I will."

Stella comes up to me and says, "Nathan, here's someone I'd like to introduce you and Marlita to. This is Tess Monaco."

"Oh my, you're the lady with the huge sunflower farm, right?" Marlita asks. "Someone told me recently that you ship gorgeous flowers all over the country."

"That's me!" she replies with a tremendous smile. "I've got a lot of acres of sunflowers ready for picking, so let me know if you want some. I'd be happy to give you as many as you want."

"Thanks, Tess," I say. "We will. We're delighted that you're so happy making other people happy."

"Well, I got a very fortunate break a while ago and just want to share some beauty in return."

We get yet another tap on our shoulders, and turn to read Hunter and Lydia Vickman's name tags.

"Oh yes, the Vickmans. The Transcend program. It's so nice to meet you. We've heard a lot of very good things about your important work preparing young kids for college."

"Thanks to helpful people like you and your wife, Nathan."

I glance at Joe as if to telepathically ask him, *"Does everyone here know that we contributed money to them?"*

Joe just smiles and shrugs his head.

After the Vickmans leave I look at my consiglieri, Joe. "So much for anonymity, right?!"

"Nathan, that ship sailed when you gave $20 million to the United Way and the Community Foundation. You didn't honestly think that would remain a secret, did you?"

I return his smile and reply, "I reckon not, but it's a little embarrassing that people know."

"Yeah, well, I'm sure you can deal with it, Nathan. The good news is that no one knows how much you and Marlita really have."

Then, we hear the melodic magic coming from Enrique Bergman's cello, and the professor nods at me as I wave back to him.

"You and he did a lot of great work together for the Greencastle Summer Music Festival, Nathan," Marlita says.

"Thanks, hon! Those days were some of my very favorite ever. Next year will be Enrique's twentieth season. He's brought musicians from virtually every corner of the world to perform at our little Asbury Chapel. Our community is so lucky to have Enrique in our midst."

And then, I'm totally shocked to see Marlita's wonderful sisters, BJ and Linda, lighting up the place with their luminous smiles, and right behind them are son, Chris, and his lovely wife, Elizabeth, along with her parents, Connie and Dave. We share hugs all around, and then the cadence of Enrique's cello music morphs into a dramatic conclusion, and we each take our seats.

"What's going on here?" I hoarsely whisper to Marlita, Stella, and Joe. "We've contributed to virtually all of these people and their organizations."

I'm about to ask for more clarification, but Marlita interjects, "Silence, darling, President Blanco is about to speak."

"But?!" I try to say.

"Just smile and act humble."

Over the course of the next half hour, President Lori Blanco and my astronomy professor friend, Morrie Kurtz, speak about Asbury College's commitment to the sciences and offer detailed specifications of the new celestial observatory's telescopes and advanced computer programs. I knew from Morrie that they were talking about making vast improvements to Asbury's physics and astronomy curricula, but I didn't know they'd gone ahead and built and furnished this magnificent silver-domed twin observatory to the McKim.

I must confess that my emotions are mixed. I mean, on the one hand this whole new stargazing facility appears to be world-class which I'm very happy about, and yet I feel a twinge of envy thinking that someone else has funded this special place. I know, it sounds petty, but as I've said before, "I'm not a perfect person."

I look at Joe and ask, "Any idea who funded this because you and I haven't talked about it?" Joe shrugs and displays ignorance.

Marlita saves Joe from having to reply further by lovingly saying, "Ssshhh, Nathan, they're still speaking."

I obediently slink back in my chair. Then, Joe gets up and begins walking to the podium.

I lean over and ask Stella: "What the fudge is going on here?!"

That earns me another, "Ssshhh! Silence!" from my loving partner.

And, Joe begins to speak. "My name's Joe Daniels. I'm an attorney from Cincinnati with the law firm of Hoffman Fabian and True. While I've had the pleasure of meeting several of you over the past year, we all have some very special friends in common."

"Oh shit!" I say to Marlita.

"Uh huh," she fawns at me. "Now it's your turn!"

Joe continues, "I know, my dear friend, Nathan Andrews, is going to shoot me for orchestrating this gathering, and I want to compliment and thank each of you for keeping this dedication so secretive. Believe me, we know how hard it is to keep a secret. The moment Marlita and Nathan decided to give the gifts to the United Way and your great community foundation, I knew that our best laid plans of charitable anonymity were out the window… and that's okay…because each us has fulfilled the tenets of our gift agreements with this fine couple."

I hear a few hoots of affirmation from Marlita's two sisters, and then Joe motions for President Blanco and Professor Kurtz to join him, and Joe turns the podium over to the president.

To this day I can't recall all of the next words that Lori Blanco spoke, and I about fainted when I saw the large sign over the entrance to the new observatory get unveiled with the words, *The Nathan and Marlita Andrews Center for Astronomy*. I'm literally in tears taking in the congratulatory scene, and the look of pride on Stella's, Joe's and our family members' faces.

After shaking a gazillion hands and getting a terrific guided tour of the new observatory by Morrie Kurtz, I finally begin to calm down a little. As a writer, I have a certain ease with words, but I find myself stammering and stuttering quite a bit at the honor and the camaraderie of the evening's celebration. I shake my finger at Joe in fake admonishment, and he, Stella, Marlita, and I give a huge, heartfelt hug.

"Congratulations, Nathan! I'm so thrilled to be a part of this," my attorney exudes, "and I can't wait to see what we do in year-two!"

He looks at Stella and says, "You've got such a loving community of friends here. I'm thinking I may need to spend even more time here if you think you could put up with me." Stella gives Joe a warm embrace. "I'm counting on it, Mr. Daniels!" she coos and plants a sweet kiss on his cheek.

Over the next several minutes, the crowd of well-wishers starts to dissipate, and I'm approached by my favorite newspaper editor, Red Jergens.

"So were you part of this friendly conspiracy, too, Red?"

"Maybe…information does have a way of flowing to me, after all, but keeping this dedication a secret from you was quite a task. Congratulations, Nathan, it couldn't happen to a more deserving guy."

"Well, it's like we talked about before, Red, all ships rise on the same tide."

Red points to the amazing new telescope situated in the gleaming Andrews Observatory and concludes, "True, Nathan! And, all ships need a steady captain at the helm, someone to help navigate the stars."

~ The End ~

Afterword

C HARITABLE GIVING is a very personal decision. A number of the nonprofit organizations
described in *Given Names* are representative of
important causes I've been personally familiar with
over the years. The following are some suggestions
of local organizations deserving support.

Beyond Homeless
beyondhomelessinc@beyondhomeless.org

Edge 21
www.edge21.org

Gobin Memorial United Methodist Church
www.gobinchurch.org

Greencastle Summer Music Festival
gsmfdirector@gmail.com

Humane Society of Putnam County
hspc14@gmail.com

Putnam County Community Foundation
pcfoundation.org

Putnam County Convention and Visitors Bureau
www.goputnam.com

Putnam County Museum
info@putnamcountymuseum.org

Putnam County Public Library
pcpl21.org

United Way of Central Indiana
www.uwci.org

"A bit of fragrance always clings to the hand that
gives roses."

About the Author
Stuart Fabe

During his adult life Stuart Fabe has enjoyed a couple of diverse but very meaningful careers, ranging from raising charitable dollars for important institutions, to creating art, and writing novels.

He began his professional life in the early 1970s working with delinquent and at-risk children who appeared in juvenile court. He then focused on organizing and conducting successful fundraising campaigns for vital organizations such as Cincinnati Children's Hospital, the Jewish Hospital, and the Cincinnati Zoo.

Throughout the decades that he raised charitable funds, Stuart always maintained a photographic darkroom where he escaped the rigors of his daily work to print fine art photographs that he exhibited at art shows and galleries throughout the Midwest.

In 2005 he moved away from Cincinnati, Ohio, to Putnam County, Indiana, to concentrate on creating art full-time, including intricate weaving on hardshell gourds and photographing the world around him and the heavens above. It wasn't until ten years ago, however, that he began writing suspense novels in a serious way. Stuart is fascinated by doing research for his books and creating intriguing stories with memorable characters.

"Given Names" is his tenth novel and begs the questions: "What would you do if you won the lottery? Who would you tell? And, what would you give away?"

He enjoys the solitude of living in the bucolic countryside near Greencastle with his life-partner, Marla, and together they contribute to the health and well-being of their family, their community, and their animals and friends.